The
Wednesday
Letters

OTHER BOOKS BY JASON F. WRIGHT

Christmas Jars

The
Wednesday
Letters

A Novel by

JASON F. WRIGHT

SHADOW
MOUNTAIN

Visit www.TheWednesdayLetters.com for book club guides, to request speaking engagements, and more.

E-mail the author at jason@thewednesdayletters.com

"Nothing Exciting" © 2007 Jason Steadman. Used by permission. For more information visit www.jasonsteadmanmusic.com

Visit us at ShadowMountain.com

Library of Congress Cataloging-in-Publication Data

Wright, Jason F.
  The Wednesday letters / Jason F. Wright.
     p. cm.
  ISBN 978-1-59038-812-9 (hardback : alk. paper)
  1. Parents—Death—Fiction.   2. Adult children—Fiction.   3. Family
secrets—Fiction.   4. Domestic fiction.   I. Title.
PS3623.R539C48 2005
813'.6—dc22   2007017056

Printed in the United States of America
R. R. Donnelley and Sons, Crawfordsville, IN

10   9   8   7   6   5   4   3   2   1

To my parents,

Willard and Sandra

Acknowledgments

Thanks, as always, to my highly biased focus group: Kodi, Beverly, Sandi Lou, Sterling, Ann, Jeff, Terilynne, John, Adrienne, Lauren, the new Jon, Wilma, Stephanie, Amanda, Marshall, Katy, Emma, Ethan, and Bailey.

And to my slightly less-biased early-draft reviewers: Monica, Kerri, Caren, Kalley, Nancy, Taylor, Ramona, Jeanette, Laurel, Matt, Christa, Laura, Janeal, Randa, Nicole, Cammy, Amanda, Cindy, and Kathi. An extra dose of thanks to Allyson Condie for reviewing more drafts than I can remember.

Thanks to the fine team at Shadow Mountain Publishing: Chris Schoebinger for his vision; Lisa Mangum for her brilliant editing; Sheryl Dickert Smith for her inspired cover design; Gail Halladay for her marketing prowess; Tonya Facemyer for her expert typesetting; Angie Godfrey for keeping my head attached; and to Sheri Dew for taking risks and raising the bar for publishing.

Thanks to my agent, Laurie Liss, for her career guidance and friendship.

A debt of gratitude is due the Schwartz and Faulkner families for offering their cabins for long, quiet writing weekends. (I looked in your medicine cabinets.)

Thanks to the many wonderful people of Woodstock, Virginia, both for their assistance in research and for welcoming my family into their community.

Loving thanks to my forgiving children, Oakli, Jadi, Kason, and Koleson for sacrificing "daddy-kid days" as I struggled to complete this novel. Meet you at W.O. Riley Park.

Thank you to my wife, Kodi, for standing by me (again), for reading draft after draft (again), for pulling much more than your share of the parenting (again), and for reminding me of Laurel Cooper in enough ways to make her real.

Finally, a hearty thanks to everyone who will read these acknowledgments and call me later to ask why I didn't thank them, too. I was protecting you; I know how easily you get embarrassed.

When in the Shenandoah Valley, please visit:
Hockman Manor House B&B (Edinburg)
Shirley at Holler Realty (Woodstock)
Walton and Smoot Pharmacy (Woodstock)
Widow Kip's Country Inn (Mount Jackson)
Woodstock Chamber of Commerce
Woodstock Tower

CHAPTER 1

APRIL 13, 1988

Wednesday Evening

Shortly after 11:00 P.M., Laurel slid under the maroon comforter and into bed next to her husband, Jack. She wrapped her strong arms around him from behind and worried at how easily she could feel his ribs. She remembered the many years when he'd weighed considerably more than she had.

Assuming Jack was already asleep, she began her nightly routine. Laurel breathed in deeply, expanding and filling every corner of her lungs. With her full lips closed tightly, she let the air slowly escape through her nose. It calmed her.

She closed her eyes; she prayed for each of her children—Matthew, Malcolm, Samantha—and for her only granddaughter, Angela, and for her only sibling, Allyson. Then she pleaded with God for more time and cursed herself for not being stronger. She ended her silent prayer with her first and last tears of the day.

"Hi." Jack's voice startled her.

1

"Hey you, I thought you were asleep." Laurel dabbed her eyes on her navy blue cotton pillowcase.

"Not quite. You feeling better?"

"I'm fine, but I'm leaving the dishes for Rain to get when she comes in tomorrow morning. I've got some heartburn still. Is it possible I'm too old for my own quesadillas?" She ran her right hand through a single, thinning patch of his grayish, silver hair and with her left hand rubbed her chest. "How 'bout you? Dizzy?"

"Nope, peachy."

"You're a horrible liar, Jack Cooper." Laurel slid her hand from his hair to his forehead.

"You're right. I blame the lump in my head." For eighteen months Laurel's seventy-one-year-old husband had fought an aggressive, inoperable brain tumor that, when discovered, was the size of a perfect shooter marble, but now resembled a Ping-Pong ball. The headaches were inconsistent; he could sometimes go two or three days without suffering. But when they returned, they brought pain, nausea, and vertigo that rendered him, for all practical purposes, tied to his bed. A bucket was never far away.

Though his doctors assured him that new drugs and therapies were rapidly being approved and readied for the market, Jack knew that nothing short of the hand of God would save him. And surely, he thought, God had better things to do than heal a small town bed-and-breakfast owner. "Like bringing peace to the Middle East or getting my Chicago Cubs back to the World Series," he liked to tell Laurel. She'd heard the joke, and at least fifty variations of it, after every doctor's appointment since his initial diagnosis.

Their Inn, dubbed by the previous owners as *Domus Jefferson—The Home of Jefferson*—rested in the heart of the Shenandoah Valley, squarely between the Allegheny and Blue Ridge Mountains. Jack often said that if he survived judgment day and his Maker granted a choice between heaven and that hillside, the inner-debate would be short.

On this spring Wednesday night, their beloved B&B was nearly empty. The only guest was Anna Belle Prestwich, wealthy heiress to a pet food manufacturing fortune. She was no doubt still awake, reading a romance novel in the $190 room for which she insisted on paying $300 a night. The room, decorated with expensive, handmade replica furniture from Thomas Jefferson's home at Monticello, overlooked the four acres of meadow sweeping from the back of the seven-bedroom Inn to the narrow creek at the forest line. When she finished three or four chapters, she'd escape outside with her husband's flashlight to walk her cat, Castro. She knew most people didn't walk cats, but most people weren't Anna Belle. And most cats didn't have weight problems.

Anna Belle had become a regular guest in the last several years, usually staying once or twice a month, though she'd been known to stay for up to ten days at a time. Her own home, a gorgeous, cavernous Southern mansion with four guesthouses—rumored by the chatty townsfolk to be worth anywhere from half a million to one hundred ten million dollars—was less than a mile away. On clear winter mornings, long after the trees had thrown their leaves to the ground, the tall silo of one of her unused barns and the roof of the white main house could be seen through the trees to the east.

The short, rotund, middle-aged Floridian met her husband, Alan Prestwich, on Miami Beach while the two were walking the shore very early one fall morning. He was collecting seashells for his secretary's daughter. Anna Belle was teaching Castro not to fear water.

Their encounter that morning led to an unlikely marriage, the first for both. Her new husband said he loved Anna Belle for being genuine, for having large, bold hips with personalities of their own, for her milky-white and buttery-smooth skin. But mostly he loved her dark red, almost maroon, and now gracefully graying hair. "The women I date," he had told her as they walked the boardwalk that first morning together, "wouldn't dare leave the house without dyeing their hair. But you, Anna Belle—you're a different fish in a sea of sameness."

"If I'm so wonderful," she answered as their first date ended, "how have all the good men eluded me?"

"They haven't. There just haven't been any good enough for you yet."

Six weeks later they were married.

During their third blissful year, Alan, the six-foot-two-inch classic American entrepreneur and freshman pilot with adventurous eyes, crashed his brand-new 1984 Gulfstream III into the Everglades on his very first solo flight. All they recovered was his seventeen-inch Maglite, shining in three feet of murky water two hundred yards from the plane's impact crater. Since then Anna Belle carried the flashlight everywhere, convinced it was a sign that some day she'd need it to find Castro in the woods after a donut binge, to fend off a black bear, or to use in some other noble effort.

Anna Belle had always been just north of overweight. When she took a job at the local A&P stocking groceries, a gaggle of cruel high school classmates began calling her just that: *A&P.* Just to spite them she happily adopted the nickname. It stuck and she never let it bother her. *Nicknames mean you matter,* she told herself. Now A&P wondered what they'd call her if they knew she'd inherited most of her husband's fortune. She was a millionaire many times over.

Not long after her husband's crash, Anna Belle picked Woodstock, Virginia, as her new home after seeing the town's name circled in ballpoint pen on a Civil War Reenactment Association brochure she found in one of her husband's filing cabinets. She was a resident less than a month later. Jack and Laurel quickly befriended their quirky new neighbor. They privately speculated that her purpose in life was to spend every penny of her wealth at their B&B.

"Guess how much A&P tipped me for her evening milk," Laurel whispered.

"A hundred."

"Higher."

"Two-fifty?"

"Higher," Laurel repeated.

"Five hundred dollars?" Jack's voice rose.

"Five hundred and nineteen dollars and fifty-two cents. Everything she had in her purse."

"That's good money for finding milk in the fridge and pouring it in a glass." He sighed and fluffed his pillow. "The woman is incorrigible."

"She's harmless."

Jack rolled over and faced his wife, looking into her experienced brown eyes. His own once-lively eyes now appeared sunken in his head an extra quarter-inch and were guarded beneath by heavy half-moon circles. He'd inherited the raccoon eyes, as Laurel teasingly called them, from his father, but in the last year the dark circles had become even darker and appeared almost separated from his cheeks. His nose almost touched hers. "One of these days we have to tell her, you know."

Ever since A&P's first visit to *Domus Jefferson,* she'd left obscenely generous tips for the most mundane services, and there was no apparent system to her generosity either. If Jack carried a bag for her, she pulled a hundred-dollar bill from her purse. If Laurel left a mint on her pillow after turning down her bed, A&P slipped several twenties into her hand at breakfast. Once, when Laurel's doctors discovered an irregular heartbeat and tracked the defect back two generations, A&P stubbornly urged her to accept money for the medical bills, even though their health insurance paid ninety-percent.

Another time, when Jack's twin brother, Joseph, was arrested on misdemeanor drug charges for the third time, A&P insisted on driving to Virginia Beach, bailing him out, and hosting him in her home because all the rooms in the B&B were booked. He stayed with her until he found work and a place of his own. Jack had been grateful to A&P and suspected the drive from Virginia Beach to Woodstock had been the longest of Joe's life.

The Coopers learned early in their relationship with A&P not to refuse her money. Their favorite guest was stubborn to a fault and would simply up the ante until they relented. Of course she had no idea they were simply giving the money to a children's shelter in southeast Washington, D.C. Without knowing it, in recent years the benevolent Anna Belle Prestwich had funded improvements to the shelter's kitchen, repaired a section of the dilapidated roof, and contributed the majority share to a new basketball court and adjoining playground with high, safe fences. There was even talk of creating a mini-library bearing her name.

"Sure, we'll tell her . . . Someday . . ." Laurel answered, but before Jack could respond, her eyes opened wide and she rolled from her side to her back, both hands grasping at her chest.

"Sweetheart!" Jack lifted his head. "What is it? Laurel? Sit up."

She struggled halfway up but fell back against the wooden headboard. "I've . . . no . . . breath . . . my chest . . . call . . ." The words were bursts of air.

Jack turned to the open window and called for A&P. "Mrs. Prestwich, come! Come quick! *Please!*"

But A&P was already on her evening walk, strolling along the creek's edge, counting stars in the reflection of the slow-moving water and chatting astrology with Castro as she tugged his leash.

"Oh, Lord, *help us!*" Jack cried out as Laurel's breathing became more pained and her eyes screamed. He looked toward the cordless phone cradle on Laurel's nightstand.

It was empty.

"My arm, Jack!" Laurel's eyes appeared to follow the pain from her chest down her left arm, past her hip, and to her foot. "Jack." She somehow made the single word sound like an apology.

"Dear Lord!" he called again.

Jack fought to sit up. He screamed into her face, "Laurel!" But neither her mouth nor her eyes responded. He swung his legs over the edge of the bed and put his feet on the floor. He could take only two steps before losing his balance and falling forward. The room spun around him and he careened into a brass floor lamp. As he tried to steady himself, the lamp gave way and he crashed on top of it, crushing the glass lampshade beneath his weight on the hardwood floor.

"Oh, Lord! Help us, Lord!" Jack lay on his back, hands flat against

the floor as he looked up at the ceiling. His head ached. Heavy tears pooled in his eyes. Turning his head to the side, his eyes found Laurel's old Tennessee license plate mounted on the far wall.

Gradually the room calmed and Jack pulled himself back onto their high, log-frame bed. Laurel's position was unchanged but her eyes were now closed. Her arms rested at her side.

"Laurel?" He put a hand on her cheek. "Sweetheart?" He placed his other hand on her quiet chest. "My sweetheart." Jack wrapped his arms around her and pulled her toward him. "My sweetheart," he said again. Carefully he rocked her listless body back and forth.

Moments later Jack tenderly placed his wife's head on her pillow.

Then from the top drawer of his nightstand, he pulled a pen, an envelope already containing several letters, and a piece of clean *Domus Jefferson* stationery. Using his King James Bible as a writing surface, he wrote:

April 13, 1988
My Dearest Laurel,

Ten minutes later Jack finished the letter, sealed it in the envelope along with the others, wrote a short note on the outside, and buried the entire stack somewhere in the New Testament. He returned the book to the nightstand, and he slid back toward his wife. Once again he carefully wedged an arm beneath her and pulled her to him. He gently brushed her soft, light-brown hair off her neck and whispered something in her still-warm ear. He kissed the corner of her forehead.

Then he thought of his son Malcolm and prayed he would survive the days ahead.

Finally, Jack gave in to his very last headache. And he slept.

It was 9:04 the next morning when a worried A&P and Castro finally pushed open the Cooper's master bedroom door. They found Jack and Laurel at peace in one another's cold arms.

CHAPTER 2

Thursday Morning

After discovering Laurel and Jack's bodies, A&P's first call was for an ambulance. While waiting ten minutes for it to arrive, she called Samantha—who wasn't answering at home—and a handful of other numbers from a sheet she discovered in Laurel's desk in the small study just off the entry parlor.

Among those first to get the news was Laurel's hairdresser, Nancy Nightbell. "Who's this? You say *who* died? Someone's dead?"

"This is A&P."

"There's no A&P's 'round here."

"Not the grocery. I'm the Cooper's neighbor, Anna Belle."

"Oh," Nancy gave words to her ah-ha moment. "Sure, the real rich lady—"

"Yes, yes," A&P interrupted. "I've got awful news—"

"Been meaning to ask," Nancy reclaimed the momentum, "who does your hair, Hon?"

"What?"

"Your hair," Nancy repeated. "Who does it? Your coloring ain't the best, Hon."

"I—"

"Oh, it don't matter," Nancy interrupted again. "You call me sometime, ya hear?"

"Yes, ma'am." The conversation was becoming a challenge, but A&P was nothing if not respectful. "I'll call."

"Now who'd you say was dead?" Nancy asked once again.

"The Coopers."

"Jack Cooper? He's gone? Rest his soul. What a good man, Jack Cooper was. Let me talk to Laurel, Hon."

"Nancy. Listen. Laurel has passed on, too. Both of them are gone."

"Both?"

"Yes."

"Jack and Laurel? Both gone?"

"Yes, ma'am, both died in the night. I found them myself."

"Oh my, oh my." Nancy took a big breath. "I'll be there in a bit, Hon." Before Nancy disconnected, A&P heard her yell in the background, "Randall! I need a ride! Turn off that dumb wrastlin' show, quit eatin' all that fudge, and git some pants on!"

On any other day A&P would have laughed.

Among the others who heard the news from Anna Belle were a fifteen-year-old girl working the morning shift at the nearby country store and gas station where the Coopers often bought supplies; the owner of the local dairy; a woman who sold advertising with a B&B newsletter in Philadelphia; a wrong number who nevertheless knew of the Coopers and through hysterical sobs promised to bring by a batch of her stuffed bell peppers; a banker in Winchester, Virginia; and Pastor Aaron Braithwaite from the non-denominational Christian church the Coopers attended in Mount Jackson.

Her final and most difficult call was to Rain Jesperson, long-time Cooper family friend and manager of *Domus Jefferson*. Unlike the Coopers, thirty-year-old Rain was a native of the Shenandoah Valley and her parents were the area's only known hippies.

Rain's country drawl was light and attractive and her shoulder-length hair was not quite blonde, but still more light and lively than brown. At just over five feet tall, she could have easily blended into a crowd. But Rain Jesperson had never blended into anything, not with eyes so green and endearing.

Rain had grown up in Strasburg, several small towns away up Route 11 North. After high school she studied advertising at James Madison University less than an hour away in Harrisonburg. While her friends moved off to the congestion of the I-95 corridor to places like Richmond, Baltimore, and New York City, Rain was content to hold to her roots. She never had any desire to leave the land she'd always called home. She liked to think her dreams could come true just as easily on the rolling hills of the Valley as in some big city, maybe even more so. Her vision hadn't changed since the long-ago nights of reading *Cinderella*: She saw a husband; she saw children; she saw a picket fence she would paint pink, not white. Mostly she saw security. Rain Jesperson believed those dreams would follow her, not the other way around.

The phone rang four times in Rain's redbrick townhouse.

"Rain?" A&P whispered.

"Yes?"

"It's A&P, Rain, over at the Inn."

"Hey, A&P, you all settled in okay? You see I bought that new organic skim milk you asked for? Have you eaten yet?"

"Yes, dear, I did. But I've—"

"We're out of the seven-grain bread, I know. I'll be in a bit later today. Laurel said I could get a few things done this morning, being that you're the only guest until late Friday."

"Rain, dear, you better head over now. Something's happened."

"Jack?" Rain asked, but didn't wait for an answer. "Jack. Okay, I'll be there in five minutes. Gosh, I had a feeling in my stomach when I left yesterday afternoon." Rain felt tears pool in her eyes. "Tell Laurel I'm coming. And bless your heart, Anna Belle, I'm sorry you had to call."

"Rain?" A&P felt nauseous.

"Yes?"

"Nothing, dear. See you soon."

Ten minutes later Rain pulled up to *Domus Jefferson.* Several police cars and an ambulance were parked in the small gravel lot, pointing at varying angles toward the front door. A&P, crying at the sight of Rain and filled with the crushing news that sat like a stone in her gut, met her at the front gate and pulled the petite woman into her big arms.

"Oh, Anna Belle, it's all right. Jack's free now, shhh." Rain's eyes filled again.

A&P withdrew from Rain's embrace enough to make eye contact. "It's Laurel. She's gone too."

Rain's arms dropped from A&P's shoulders. "What do you mean, *gone?*"

"Passed away," A&P choked. "Laurel's passed away too."

Rain pushed open the wooden gate and ran up the cobblestone path toward the steps and porch guarding the Inn's oversized front door. She never saw the small circles of people hugging and crying as they gathered on the yard and on the porch.

"Laurel?" Rain yelled as she stepped into the foyer. Two policemen and a third man in a suit stood against the wall talking quietly. "Laurel?" Rain ran up the stairs, pushing past another officer at the top.

"Ms. Jesperson, please, downstairs please." He reached to stop her, catching an inch of her sleeve but losing it when Rain tore free and threw open the master bedroom door. Inside a woman was taking pictures of a broken lamp and its shattered shade. A heavy white sheet covered a mound in the center of the bed.

"Rain." A&P appeared in the doorway, speaking softly but in control. "They've both died, Sweetheart, in the night."

"Laurel? How? An accident?" Rain's knees wobbled and she moved to sit on a chair just inside the door, but the county's free-lance crime photographer caught her, apologized twice, and asked if they'd please return downstairs.

At the kitchen table A&P replayed the series of events leading to her discovery of the couple's bodies shortly after nine that morning.

"I don't believe it," Rain said, but knowing in her heart it was true.

"They don't know for sure, but Laurel probably had a stroke or heart attack in bed. I guess Jack went for help, but it was too late. And you know he'd been really suffering, even went up to bed pretty early last night. I guess he just stopped living, you know?"

Rain nodded and sipped on a glass of water.

"They were just lying there in bed together, curled up happy as can be." A&P slid her chair closer to Rain's. "They looked like a greeting card. You know those kind they have at Hallmark? The black-and-white photos of people in love and on the inside it's just blank so you can write your own message in your own words? You know the way they always look? It's like nothing could ever be wrong. Like that's the way they'd want the world to end. That's how Jack and Laurel looked. Jack's face was as handsome as ever. So comfortable. So peaceful." She paused and turned her gaze to the window. "I wish that's how my Alan had died."

Both women were breathing more calmly, looking out the kitchen window at the growing crowd in the front yard. While Rain's eyes were on the gathering mourners, her mind was on Malcolm Cooper.

CHAPTER 3

M other and Father are dead."

"What? Sammie?" Malcolm yelled into his satellite phone.

"They're gone, Mal." Malcolm's younger sister, Samantha, repeated the news and reached for her .357 sitting on the kitchen counter. She spun the cylinder with her strong, callused hands and spoke into the seventy-six-year-old wood and polished brass Western Electric wall telephone. She spoke with purpose, firm but weary after a draining morning that featured seeing her parents zipped into black bags, removed from *Domus Jefferson,* and transported to the county morgue. She eyed a cushioned bar stool beyond her reach, half-hidden underneath another counter along the other side of the oversized kitchen.

"*How,* Sammie? *How* are they gone?"

"Mom had a heart attack, Mal, and Dad went with her. Last night sometime."

Malcolm watched a sapajou monkey take a drink from the

river's edge. A twelve-foot snake slid atop the water just a few feet away.

"Mother?"

"Yes."

"And Dad?"

"He had cancer, Malcolm."

"I didn't know," he said quietly. Malcolm switched the heavy phone from one ear to the other and looked west toward the skyline. Trees and deep green vines soared high, sneaking into the sky that guarded the jungles and Amazon River in Manaus, Brazil. He took a single, heavy flat stroke through the moss-covered water and twisted the wooden ore vertically, just enough to guide his silver, fourteen-foot, flat-bottom boat back toward the heart of the world's second longest river. His eyes filled with tears for his mother.

"I'll come home," he finally said.

"You will?" Samantha asked.

"I'll need a day or two."

"You sure, Malcolm? We'll have to tell him you're coming."

"I'm sure. I'll be there," he insisted. "Wait for me."

"All right."

"I'm sorry, Sam."

"Me too," she whispered.

"I'm sorry I'm not there already." He choked out the words.

"It's all right, Mal, you did what you did. It's all right."

Malcolm took three deep breaths.

"I love ya. You know that, Sis?"

"I know. Me too."

"You love yourself?"

"Oh, shut it." Samantha chuckled for the first time since hearing on her police cruiser scanner that there were two DBs at *Domus Jefferson*.

Samantha pulled on the antique phone's lever to disconnect and placed another call. "He's on his way," she told her oldest brother, Matthew.

"From where?"

"No idea." Samantha exhaled. "Nature, I imagine."

"How long?"

"He said two days."

"Then he's still in Brazil, I bet." Matthew paused then asked, "How did he take it?"

"Quietly."

"Figures."

Neither his parents nor his siblings had spoken to Malcolm in almost a year. An occasional postcard from a remote location in South America was usually all they received since his sudden departure from Woodstock two years earlier. He'd last called a few days after opening a care package his mother sent to his apartment in Sete Lagoas, Brazil. The box contained Laurel's no-bake cookies, a note from Rain Malcolm packed away but never read, and some cash from A&P hidden in several pair of tube socks. Malcolm used the cash on clay water filters, children's shoes, and even managed to stretch the money far enough to include a handful of picture books.

The package also contained an expensive satellite phone. A Post-It was stuck to the instruction manual. Written in his mother's neat cursive handwriting was, "Be safe. Call when you're ready." He called, but that first conversation ended when she begged him to return home. She regretted not having time to tell him his father was dying. Malcolm carried the phone everywhere but rarely turned it on.

"How's Dad's list coming?" Samantha asked Matthew.

"Good—I've called everyone. Three or four names I didn't recognize, but A&P helped me find numbers. Hopefully they all make it."

"Hope so."

"Oh," Matthew remembered, "Aunt Allyoon called me back. She wasn't able to get a flight from Vegas until Saturday afternoon."

"Can't wait to see her. Gosh, it's been years."

"A couple. She came out for Mom and Dad's thirty-fifth, remember?" Matthew paused. "I take it still no word from Dad's brother?"

"He's our *uncle*," Samantha answered, not shielding her annoyance. "And no, not yet. I left another message with his parole officer in St. Louis."

"Don't quote me, Sis, but I won't lose sleep if he doesn't come. Malcolm will pack along enough drama."

21

"Maybe," Samantha said, "but he's got to know."

"Fair. Keep trying."

Samantha knew what would come next.

"You called Nathan yet?" Matthew asked.

"You know it's not that easy."

"I know, Sam, but he's the Commonwealth's Attorney. He's got to know Malcolm's coming back. Do you want to ask Rain to tell him?"

"I guess I can do that." She finally holstered her revolver. "She's taken it hard, Matt. Real hard."

"I bet," he replied. "She there yet?"

"Got here a bit ago. She's outside with Anna Belle and some of the neighbors."

"Poor Rain, might as well be family."

"Might as well."

"You tell her I said 'thank you' for all the help, would you? I've got a flight into Dulles. I'll get a car and drive straight down. I should be at the Inn between five and six."

"Is Monica coming?"

"No, she can't. Her business is taking off and she just can't get away."

"Can't get away?"

"No."

"I'm sorry, Matt. Everything okay with you guys?"

"Oh, yeah, we're fine. You know Monica—she'd be thinking

about her clients the whole time anyway. She's taking this thing pretty seriously, twenty-four-hour service, you know the drill. And it's all so new, the stress of going out on her own, it's hard for her."

"Matt, she's a personal trainer—"

"Life coach."

"—Whatever. She could get away. You know it. You *need* her right now."

"It's fine, Sam, really. Plus, we had a big meeting scheduled with that adoption guru and another mother in Newark this week-end. This could be it, for real this time. She didn't want to miss it. The timing's just not good."

"Be sure to tell that to Mom and Dad. They should have died in another couple weeks." Samantha's voice rose and cracked. "I'm sorry. . . . It'll be good to see you."

"You too, Sam. I'm sorry I'm not already there."

She nodded. "I know." Tears ran.

"Sam?"

"Yeah?"

"We're going to make it."

"I hope so."

"Sam?"

"Yeah, Matt?"

"Talk to Rain."

She breathed. "I will."

CHAPTER 4

Thursday Evening

B *oa tarde,"* Malcolm told the young woman sitting at the TAM Brazilian Airlines ticket counter.

"Boa tarde, senhor."

"Eu preciso passagem para Washington, D.C."

"Fala inglês?" the young brunette asked.

"I do. Do I look American?" He ran his fingers through his rough beard. Malcolm's skin was tanned and weathered from months of living in the Amazon and his eyes were sore and deep red. His hair stopped just off his shoulders.

"Yes, sir." She smiled, revealing brilliant white teeth that contrasted beautifully with her naturally dark complexion. "You need travel to United States. What day?"

"As soon as possible—today if I can."

"Last flight to Miami depart in twenty-five minutos . . . minutes, excuse me . . . but you will not pass customs in such little time."

"Los Angeles?"

"Tonight? No." She shook her head. "Wait please." She deftly slipped her long black hair behind her ears.

Malcolm noticed two small birthmarks previously hidden near the top of her neck, just below her jawline under her right ear.

She tapped feverishly on an archaic beige keyboard. "We fly you to Rio and you lay over and catch straight flight to Miami. Then in Miami you fly to Washington Dulles. That is final destination?"

"Close enough, yes."

"That is in Virginia, *correto*?" she asked. "It is beautiful in Virginia?"

"What?" Malcolm asked, distracted.

"I'm sorry," she offered, embarrassed. "Then I enter the order? You land in Washington two hours earlier than by waiting for the first flight from here tomorrow morning."

"Two hours is all?"

"*Sim.* Two hours."

Malcolm admired her youthful, innocent face. The florescent lights would have been unflattering to anyone else, but for the angelic young Brazilian they made her bronze skin glow. He imagined she was twenty-one, maybe twenty-two. Though he'd been tempted by a dozen women during his time in Brazil, his mother's Christian, cautious voice, and the image of Rain's memory, had persuaded him to resist.

He felt again the shock of loss move through him, followed quickly by a reckless sense of abandon. This young lady was as stunning as any woman he'd met in Brazil. He leaned on the counter. "What about Plan B?"

"Plan B? What is a Plan B?"

"Plan B. I stay here and watch you work until your shift ends. Then I buy you dinner, we walk along the river, and you say good-bye to me at"—Malcolm leaned further over the counter and turned his head enough to see the monitor—"at 7:32 A.M., just as I board flight 2122 for Miami."

The girl smiled and subtly looked left and right. "Yes, sir. I say I would like this Plan B."

"Then book it." Malcolm smiled back and handed her a wad of Brazilian *reais* from his knapsack.

The girl verified Malcolm's passport and handed him a small folder containing his boarding pass, change, receipt, and customs forms. "I'm Ana Paula," she whispered, stretching her hand across the counter.

"Malcolm. *Prazer em conhecê-la.*" He shook her hand with both of his.

"Nice to meet you, too." She turned to see her shift supervisor watching from three ticket windows away, suddenly aware of the lingering American expressing interest in his brand-new employee. "I am done at ten o'clock tonight. I meet you at taxi stand."

"Ten o'clock," he repeated playfully in her accent.

"Next?" Ana Paula called to an overweight Italian woman waiting in the rope line. Behind her Malcolm disappeared and began passing the hours until his rendezvous with the Brazilian beauty.

A few minutes after ten Ana Paula appeared as promised at the taxi station outside the airport terminal.

Malcolm sat on a nearby bench fiddling nervously with his satellite phone and watching taxi drivers scrum over Caucasian passengers. His stomach churned.

Ana Paula wore thin pink shorts and a white tank top with yellow straps. Her black hair spilled over her smooth, rounded shoulders.

Malcolm stared, his lips slightly apart. *I may never be here again,* he thought.

"*Oi.*"

"Hello," she answered.

"So which does the lovely Ana Paula prefer, English or Portuguese?"

"Truly? I prefer English. I don't have practice you know. I attend a school at night but not many friends here at airport speak English. They think they do because they say *Mac Donald's* and *Pizza Hoot.* But I do not think that counts."

"Ha!" Malcolm stood to meet her eyes. "You are correct." He bent down and grabbed his army-style duffle bag and knapsack. "Let's eat."

"*Mac Donalds?*" she giggled.

"*Feijoada.*"

"*Sério?*"

"*Sério.* It might be my last meal in Brazil for some time."

"Oh?"

"But I'm here tonight."

Her smile returned. "A taxi then. We go to restaurant at Hotel Tropica on the river. You have been?"

"No, but do they have *feijoada*?"

She giggled again. "I am sure, yes. It is one of the finest restaurants in Manaus."

Malcolm grabbed her hand and pulled her toward a cab. Stepping in front of an older American couple, he slid into the backseat with his bag and, in a rush, pulled Ana Paula on top of his lap. "Hotel Tropica," he said as the driver peeled away.

At 11:15 they were served *feijoada*: a heavy Brazilian stew packed with beans, vegetables, pork hoofs, ears, and a snout. It was leftover from that afternoon's lunch special and served only upon Malcolm's guarantee of a generous gratuity.

In the following hours they talked of Ana Paula's dream of studying in the United States and of her recent surprise birthday party, her eighteenth.

By 1:30 A.M., Malcolm had revealed the purpose of his emergency trip home to Virginia and the trouble that awaited him. He had even spoken of his novel, the one he'd been writing for more years than he cared to remember. Malcolm explained how he planned to celebrate the night his book first appeared on the *New York Times* bestseller list. Once he finished it, of course.

What he didn't reveal was Ana Paula's role in helping Malcolm flush Rain's image from his mind before seeing her face again.

Meanwhile, with her index, middle, and ring fingers, Ana Paula drew figure eights on the exposed underside of Malcolm's arm that he draped across the cream-colored linen tablecloth. From moment to moment Malcolm worked earnestly to force the death of his parents from his mind just long enough to enjoy her touch.

Sometime around 2:30, in an empty bar adjacent the four-star restaurant, the couple finished a second bottle of wine as a lone janitor mopped the floors around them.

Ana Paula leaned forward and whispered something, her lips hanging an extra second on his ear. Her smell was intoxicating—and familiar. But when Malcolm looked back into her gorgeous brown eyes, he saw someone else.

"I can't." The answer surprised them both.

And at 7:00, despite saying no to the Brazilian beauty, Malcolm boarded flight 2122 with his mother's voice in his head and his gut full of guilt.

CHAPTER 5

Friday Morning

On his flight to Miami, Malcolm stared not out, but into the window next to him. In his reflection he saw his mother, Laurel, dancing alone in the spacious living room on the day his parents closed on their purchase of *Domus Jefferson*. The Inn had been freshly painted white, every inch of it, a condition Jack had placed on the sale. It was summer, 1968. Malcolm was thirteen years old.

Somewhere in the house Malcolm's older brother, Matthew, was grilling his father with questions about the profitability of running a bed-and-breakfast and the wisdom of leaving the security of his position as head of maintenance at the University of Virginia. It was hardly a position of great prestige, Matthew admitted, but it was a comfortable, reliable paycheck and a reward for twenty-two years of service to the University in a variety of blue-collar jobs. Jack's coworkers often called him *Jack Barry,* both for his resemblance to the host of the game show *Twenty-One,* and for his love of trivia.

"You got to be the smartest head of maintenance in the public university system," Jack's friends said. "You ought to be running the operation up at Yale. You're the best-read toilet expert in America." They teased, he laughed, they teased even more, and he smiled knowing he'd have the last laugh. He did.

Jack and Laurel had been quietly saving for the dream of owning their own B&B for ten years, but they expected the dream to materialize after the children had grown and left home. Then a windfall—a six-figure gift—from Jack's dying uncle in Pittsburgh accelerated their plans.

Though Jack and Laurel didn't have to, they arranged for an apartment for Jack's twin brother, Joe, with a prepaid six-month lease and several thousand dollars to support himself while he found yet another job. Just weeks before the Coopers closed on the purchase of the Inn, Joe was fired from a landscaping job with Albemarle County. Apparently, they didn't appreciate him driving a riding mower four miles downtown for a drink during his lunch break.

"Drink, sir?" The flight attendant's soft voice startled him. Malcolm shook his head and pulled down the plane's window shade. He'd never been a good sleeper. He turned off his overhead lamp, rested his head against the window, and let his eyes fall shut.

In his memory he saw Samantha, his chronically moody sister. She was reading Shakespeare on the front porch and wondering how long to wait before asking permission to make another long distance call. The melodramatic ten-year-old was still unhappy about leaving her friends in Charlottesville and relocating north to Virginia's Shenandoah Valley. "At least Charlottesville was just sleepy," she complained to her parents. "This place is downright groggy."

Though in time Samantha adjusted to Woodstock and made a quirky collection of new friends, she always missed the life she'd left behind in the eclectic town that Thomas Jefferson built. She took solace in the small, two-bedroom cottage that sat fifty yards from the main house and in which she and Malcolm would live until they finished high school.

Despite the freedom and perks of the cottage—which some loved and others hated her for, but all envied—Samantha continued to miss Charlottesville. In particular she missed the many community theaters and frequent opportunities to audition for stage shows. Samantha had been appearing on stage in mostly minor roles since she was just six but was already seasoned enough to say the theater scene in the Shenandoah Valley was "amateurish, uninspiring, and unbefitting someone with so much raw potential." She threatened more than once to leave Virginia altogether, hitchhike the hundred miles into Washington, D.C., take Amtrak to

New York City, and take her shot on Broadway. On her seventeenth birthday, she did just that.

Matthew, the oldest of the three Cooper children, was seventeen the year the family moved to Woodstock and, thanks to two summers of all-day summer school in Charlottesville, was scheduled to graduate from high school a full year early. Despite the advice from his father that he enroll in school his senior year to enjoy his adolescence and play football for the Falcons of Woodstock's Central High, Matthew had long since burned out on sports. He was anxious to attend college at Virginia Tech in Blacksburg and begin studying business. Worried about disappointing his father, the three-sport all-star blamed a bad knee for his premature exit from sports. Matthew thought his father dreamt of his son making millions. And yes, Matthew dreamt of riches, but he wanted to earn them on Wall Street, not on a football field.

Malcolm could picture that summer night more clearly now than the night he lived it. His mother wore a light yellow sundress and swayed back and forth to an Elvis record playing on the vintage record player that came with the Inn. He watched from the large dining room table.

"That's not dancing, Mom."

"Oh it's not, Malcolm Cooper?"

"Even Sammie dances better than that."

"Shut it, doofus," Samantha called through the open window from the porch.

"Samantha!"

"Sorry, Mother—*doof.* Better?"

Laurel suppressed a laugh.

"Would you care to put on your dancing shoes, young Mr. Cooper?" his mother challenged.

"Fine, but just one song," he said as he passed by the front door and into the living room. "Pay attention, Sammie," he yelled. "You might learn something."

"Like how to puke on my shoes?"

"Back to your book, Samantha. And you knock that sass off, Mister." Laurel squinted one eye playfully and held her hands out. "Shall we dance?"

For three songs Malcolm and his mother moved around the living and dining rooms, fluidly circling the table like it was another couple on the dance floor, and eventually passing through the kitchen.

"You *are* quite the dancer!" Laurel squealed as she bent down low to spin under his arm. "You're even better than advertised!"

The words might not have meant any more if God himself had spoken them.

"Ladies and gentlemen," the Brazilian flight attendant spoke English with less of an accent than most natives Malcolm had met during his time in Brazil. "We're beginning our final descent into the Miami area. The captain has asked that you turn off and stow all portable electronic devices and return your trays to the upright and locked position. Local time is 3:30 P.M."

Malcolm handed three empty pretzel bags and a Sprite can to the flight attendant and pulled the airsickness bag from the seat pouch in front of him, just in case.

Across the aisle from him sat two Brazilian boys—probably twins Malcolm guessed—and a man Malcolm assumed was the boys' father, who was sitting between them in the middle seat reading a soccer magazine. The boys leaned in and pointed at players. They argued playfully over who was better. "Shh," the father said. *"Fecham suas bocas."* He looked at Malcolm and smiled.

Malcolm's eyes fell shut again and found a dirt and grass soccer field next to an unusually well-adorned chapel in Sete Lagoas. He'd been walking home from lunch through the plaza downtown, an area that featured restaurants, bars, and bakeries just feet from one of the seven lakes that gave the Brazilian town its name. His belly was full with black beans and rice and thinly sliced strips of steak. He could still taste the sweet bubbles of soda—the berry-flavored Guaraná—on his tongue.

"Oi, amigo!" A boy yelled. *"Americano! Americano!"*

Malcolm looked over.

"Quer jogar?"

Malcolm smiled broadly and pointed to his flip-flops. *"Não tenho sapatos,"* he said. *"Não tenho sapatos."*

The boy laughed and half a dozen other players gathered, staring at the tall, white American.

"Olha!" one of them yelled and each of the boys pointed to his own feet.

Malcolm hadn't noticed: half wore sandals, half wore no shoes at all. Malcolm smiled again, walked onto the field, and kicked off his flip-flops. One of the boys gestured for him to take off his shirt and join the *skins* team. He did, and within seconds it seemed, the skies unloaded a month's worth of rain.

They played on.

Malcolm ran up and down the field until his legs burned, chasing the ball and the boys as if he were twelve. The boys danced around him and glided with the ball as they moved in rhythm across the field. When Malcolm had a breakaway opportunity, the goalie appeared to slip in the rain and Malcolm scored. He was sure the boy had slipped on purpose.

Malcolm winked at him.

The boy winked back.

Soaked with rain and covered with mud, Malcolm grabbed his shirt and fell to his back near midfield. The boys pounced on top of him and peppered him with questions about the U.S.

Was he rich? What color was the sky in America? Had he been to a 7–11? Was he married? Do American dogs bark in English? Would he take them all home with him? Just one?

Malcolm patiently answered each boy and before leaving,

pulled a wet wad of bills from his front pocket. He handed it to one of the boys and pointed to a bakery across the street. The boys yelped and screamed with delight. Some shook his hand, others said, "High five! High five!"

Another simply said, *"Obrigado,"* and gave Malcolm a long hug.

It was that boy's dirty, grateful face in Malcolm's mind when the boys next to him on the flight to Miami erupted into loud laughter and were again reprimanded by their father. Malcolm turned and looked out over the ocean.

My parents are dead, he thought.

He was a few hours and one more flight away from an awkward reunion with Matthew and Samantha, a funeral for two, and a confrontation with the memories of his father. His mind spun.

Malcolm shook from his mind the even more awkward reunion with the authorities he'd run from and the man who'd stolen the love of his youth.

My parents are dead.

Despite it all, he could smell Rain's perfume already.

CHAPTER 6

Friday Evening

"Is he here yet?" Nathan Crescimanno bellowed as he climbed out of his BMW and moved toward the front gate of *Domus Jefferson*.

"Not yet," Samantha answered, standing alone on the porch. At five-foot-two inches and wearing a suit slightly too big for him, Samantha thought Nathan resembled a boy borrowing his father's car. He wore John Lennon-style gold-rimmed glasses.

"Where's Rain?"

"Inside. But keep your voice down, would you? There's a lot going on."

"Where's Matthew?"

"Inside. What is this, Nathan? Interrogation?"

"Sorry. I'm significantly wound up." Nathan instinctively scratched the bridge of his nose. "Would you get Matt for me, please? I'll stay out here."

Samantha nodded, her eyes smiling, and stepped into the

crowded Inn. Moments later she trailed Matthew back onto the porch.

"Hey, Nathan," Matthew said, shaking his hand firmly and remembering how small and soft Nathan's hands were for a man.

"Matt, Matt, Matt, you made it in. How's it going? How's Boston?"

"Boston's great, but I'm actually in New Yo—"

"And where's that gorgeous woman of yours? Mon not coming down?"

"No, Monica isn't coming. Business is booming for her right now."

"Good for her. Hey, Matt, I'm sorry about your folks. I know this is tough."

Across the porch, Samantha turned and rolled her eyes.

"I appreciate that. . . . So what's the latest? You talk to Chief Romenesko?"

"I did, and like I promised you on the phone, I made it happen. We're going to look the other way until the funeral is over. I convinced him Malcolm wouldn't be a risk to run . . . for a few days anyway."

"I appreciate that," Matthew said. "*We* appreciate that," Matthew repeated, looking toward his sister.

She forced a thankful nod in Nathan's general direction.

The screen door opened and Rain appeared.

"Hey there!" Nathan said. "You okay? I tried to call here fifty times today. Why didn't you answer?"

"I'm sorry, Nathan, we just couldn't get every call, the phone's been ringing off the hook."

Nathan moved toward her and pulled her close. "It's okay," he said with tenderness reserved only for her. "I've just been worried."

"I know," she said, releasing the tension and squeezing his shoulders. "I'm sorry."

"We're going to be okay, babe." He raised his voice enough to be heard across the porch. "This will all be over soon."

"I'm going back in," said Samantha, and then she appeared to mask something under a loud cough.

Matthew looked at his shoes and smiled.

"Rain, love, why don't you follow her back in, I need to wrap up a few things with Matthew in private." He leaned close and kissed her cheek. "Love you," he whispered.

Rain smiled warmly, hugged him again, stepped back into the house, and followed Samantha upstairs.

"So listen, Matt, I've got to stay close the next few days until this all wraps up. I'll probably ask Sammie to help as well to, you know, keep an eye on Malcolm. He shouldn't be left alone."

"Understood, Nathan. And I appreciate you letting us do this quietly. Losing both our folks in one night is traumatic enough for us. We don't need more disruptions than absolutely necessary. It will be a trying couple of days."

"Naturally. And listen, Rain and I will stay out of the way as best we can." Nathan worked to sound authoritative. "And I trust you'll be around when Malcolm shows?"

"Should be."

"And where are you staying?"

Matthew tilted his head slightly and furrowed his thick eyebrows into one. "I'm staying here, Nathan, it's a B&B."

"Right." He sheepishly turned to examine the house as if seeing it for the first time. "Well, I better get inside."

"Nathan?" Matthew called just as Nathan put his hand on the screen door.

"Yeah?"

"Wedding still on?"

"You heard?"

"Of course."

"Why do you ask? You know something I don't?" Nathan laughed nervously; Matthew thought it sounded less like a laugh and more like croup.

"Relax, I just didn't know. Living in New York keeps me a little out of the Woodstock loop. Sam just mentioned the Inn was hosting your reception and I put two and two together. Reception. Wedding."

"Clever. Yes, it's on. Unless something comes up, right?"

"Right." Matthew nodded.

"Just keep an eye on your brother."

In the master bedroom, tidied as though it hadn't ever witnessed two deaths, Samantha and Rain laid on the king-sized bed looking up at the slowly spinning ceiling fan.

"I still can't believe it," said Rain.

"I know."

"Your mom and dad are gone. Just like that."

"I know. It's like a dream. I keep thinking Dad's just out walking the property or reading in the study. But I've checked. He's gone."

"I ache so much, and I'm just a friend here, just an employee—"

"Rain," Samantha interrupted, "you know you are more than that. You're family. Mom and Dad loved you."

"I hope so." Rain wiped the beginnings of tears from the corners of her eyes with her thumbs. "I'm already sick of crying, and it's only been twenty-four hours. We've got another couple days of this."

"I know it." Samantha took a long, audible breath. "Have you thought about what you're going to do?" She turned her head toward Rain.

"About?"

"You know what about."

"About my job here? About the Vanatter reception scheduled for next weekend? About my gutters? I've almost got a Christmas tree growing—"

"You know what I mean."

"Oh."

"Yeah, oh."

"You mean what am I going to do about that guy. What's-his-name—the wanderer?"

"That's the one."

Rain smiled weakly. "I haven't gotten that far. Honestly, my head is Jell-O here, Sam. I'm still trying to figure out what's happened."

"Are you lying to a police officer?" Samantha swatted Rain's hip with the back of her hand.

"I don't know. Sure, I guess it's crossed my mind a time or two—or a hundred—but none of those thoughts have led me anywhere but sick."

"He'll be here tonight, you know. Called me from Miami."

"How's he getting here?"

"Rental car. He wouldn't take me up on a ride. I would have walked all the way down there and carried him back if it meant getting out of here for a few hours."

"Oh, no, are there too many people downstairs? Want me to start sending folks away?"

"No, no, they mean well," Samantha said, "but it's draining. I'm hugged out." They laid silently for a beat. "You know you can't avoid him for three days."

"I know." Rain resigned herself. Another minute passed.

Samantha finally asked the question Rain feared most. "You still love him"—she paused—"don't you?"

Rain twisted her engagement ring around her finger. "I'm practically married, Sam."

"That's not what I asked."

"I love Nathan. I do. He's sweet to me, treats me like a princess most of the time. I know he rubs some people the wrong way, I see it, I do. But he's a gentleman to me. He's so solid, so patient with me. He loves me. He has dreams."

"Dreams of running the world."

"Not the world, Sam, just the Commonwealth of Virginia. And, might I add, he lives in the same zip code I do. That makes it a lot easier to court."

"Now listen here, it's not as if you gave the Wanderer much of a reason to stay." Samantha turned her head toward Rain and apologized with her eyes.

They laid silently and listened to the murmurs downstairs and the front door opening and closing seemingly every minute or two.

"Sam?"

"Yeah?"

"Speaking of dreams . . ."

"Uh-oh," Samantha mumbled.

"What about yours? What now?"

"I've had dreams, some really big ones I think, but they've been put on a shelf for a while." She hesitated. "You know how it is." Samantha stared back at the ceiling.

"Why'd you quit?"

"Acting?"

"Yes."

"Oh, I don't know. Will hated that life. Hated the other actors. He thought they all wanted to take his place in my life. Thought all actors were shallow and selfish."

"But you weren't."

"I hope not."

"But he was, wasn't he?"

"In more ways than one," Samantha said emphatically.

Rain slapped Samantha's leg. "So why not now?"

"Oh, maybe someday, I guess. I don't have buckets of time right now."

Rain considered her response. "But you might, in time, find more time. And I bet they'd love to see you back at the troupe in Harrisonburg."

"Maybe."

"What's it been?" Rain asked. "Five years? Seven?"

"Something like that."

Rain rubbed her eyes then stretched her arms above her head. "You know I'll be first in line. First ticket. First row. First show."

"I know," Samantha said. "But let's get you fixed first."

"Oh, brother. How do you have time to worry about the affairs of my heart in the middle of all this?"

"It's therapeutic. Look, I think I'm pretty much ninety-nine-percent numb. There is nothing in my manual for dealing with the death of your mom and dad on the same night. So I guess thinking about your troubles helps make mine seem a little easier." She turned to Rain again and smiled.

"Samantha Cooper!" Rain grabbed the extra pillow between them and whacked Samantha in the head.

"Shhh, there are mourners downstairs." The two women stifled an exhausted laughter.

"Sam, what am I going to do?"

"I dunno. I really don't."

They rested quietly until the noise below them moved outside and into the yard, then into the small parking lot, and eventually was divided up into a dozen cars.

The Inn was quiet.

CHAPTER 7

M alcolm looked down at a stack of local-area maps. "I've just flown in from South America for a funeral," he told Salima, the woman working the swing shift at the Avis counter. The kindly, pleasant-looking young woman upgraded him from an economy to a midsize. When he added that the funeral was for not one, but *both* of his beloved parents, she upgraded him to a full-size. Then, after confiding that the only woman he'd ever loved had left him two years earlier and he was terrified to see her again, he drove off the lot in a dark blue Mustang convertible.

It was unseasonably warm for Virginia, even for mid-April; the dashboard thermometer read seventy-one degrees. He pulled into the emergency lane on the highway onramp and put the Mustang's top down.

Malcolm drove west through suburban northern Virginia until the strip malls and fast food joints slowly faded into farmland and rolling hills along Route 66 and later south on 81. Less than three hours after landing at Dulles, he stood in a gas station at the Wood-stock exit buying a Diet Coke and two boxes of Tic Tacs. He was relieved, and more than a little surprised, that the clerk behind the register was a face he'd never seen before.

He put the top up on the Mustang before pulling out of the gas station and heading for town. Little had changed in the two years he'd been gone. Earlier he'd noticed a new Arby's at the free-way exit and a nicely remodeled Shell station, but downtown Woodstock looked precisely as it had two years ago when he had run out of town with clothes in one bag and a free plane ticket in his pocket.

Walton & Smoot's Drug Store was dark. So, too, was the gift shop next door and the Century 21 office on the corner. A block further down on Main Street, Devin Rovnyak's family-owned movie theater had a few lights on, and Malcolm guessed Devin's twin teenage sons were inside with their friends watching next week's release. He wondered if they'd left the back door open. For old time's sake he could sneak in and scare them from behind wear-ing a jumbo popcorn bucket over his head and wildly wielding two pairs of hotdog tongs. He was sure one of the twins would wet his pants in front of whomever he was trying to impress; Mal-colm had seen it before. *Tempting,* he thought. *Maybe another night.*

Malcolm drove to the far end of town and pulled into the Ben Franklin Department Store parking lot and was reminded again why he loved Woodstock. Unlike many Virginia towns,

Woodstock was neither a complete throwback to another century nor an entirely new and modern community. In the parking lot of the Ben Franklin—surely one of the last still standing—sat a brand-new branch of a national bank. Historic sites peered across the main drag at new restaurants and hotel chains. Malcolm considered it the perfect blend of old and new. The locals would never forget their town's rich heritage or sacrifice their safe, small-town spirit. But neither would they resist, just out of principle, a Wendy's Double with Cheese and a large Frosty.

Malcolm pulled the convertible onto Route 11 and drove the other way back through town. He turned left onto Woodstock Tower Road and followed it several miles up the winding mountain and into the George Washington National Forest. Just a few minutes later, at the peak of the mountain overlooking Woodstock and the famous Seven Bends of the Shenandoah River, Malcolm hiked a hundred yards up the rocky trail to the well-known metal tower. He climbed up its ladder and stepped onto its generous platform.

Malcolm and his high school rat pack had spent many hours atop Woodstock Tower. It offered a unique, panoramic view of northern Virginia. To the west, from the one-time fire observation station, visitors saw Woodstock and the Seven Bends of the North Fork of the Shenandoah River. To the east, if the air was crisp and clear, one could see Fort Valley and Massanutten Mountain. The clearest of days offered glimpses of the Blue Ridge Mountains. He made a mental note to return to the tower during the daylight to enjoy the view.

Malcolm shined his flashlight over the metal roof and smiled at the graffiti. Some was new; some was familiar. He saw his own handwriting still scrawled on one of the support poles in red Sharpie: I LOVE RJ.

Malcolm drove back down the narrow, gravel road to Route 11. He drove south again and noticed a light was on upstairs in the town's museum. He wondered if Maria Lewia had finally retired. She'd been his high school English teacher and was the primary reason he'd wanted to become a novelist. She had published a few novels of her own; one had even been a steamy romance novel written under a pseudonym. Mrs. Lewia finally retired from teaching when she realized she could no longer verbally wrestle with seventeen-year-olds. Her retirement lasted less than one week. Bethany Brickhouse, a remarkably fit and good-looking eighty-two-year old, had been the longtime director of the museum and was easily its most generous donor. One year Mrs. Brickhouse collapsed in the heat and humidity at Central High's graduation and never regained consciousness. After being prodded by the mayor, members of the town council, her neighbors, and even Malcolm himself, Mrs. Lewia assumed Mrs. Brickhouse's place as museum director.

Despite the late hour, Malcolm considered pulling over and paying a visit to his writing mentor, but he thought better of it.

Mrs. Lewia would ask if he'd ever finished his novel. He hadn't. Plus the last thing she would need, or any other senior citizen for that matter, was an accident a la the Rovnyak twins.

He rolled further along and stopped in front of Woody's bar. It was quiet for a Friday night. High school football season was long over; there was no game to celebrate.

Malcolm hadn't been anywhere near the bar since the last time he saw Rain. Looking at the sidewalk, remembering that night, seeing in his memory a red tooth roll to a stop on a manhole cover made his weak stomach spin.

He remembered his visit to Rain's townhouse in the early-morning hours after the fight. He'd stood at her front door and told her that the man he'd savaged that night was the son of a prominent Virginia lawmaker, and Malcolm was sure he'd be punished beyond fairness and reason for the fight. Malcolm told her that the fight would be the final blot on his already checkered record. He told her that Nathan had bragged that their engagement was official. *Is it true?* he'd demanded to know. He told her she needed time and distance between herself and the man Malcolm knew couldn't be trusted. He begged her to leave Woodstock with him.

Rain held up a bare finger and tearfully accused Malcolm of once again allowing jealousy to reign over him.

Malcolm begged.

Rain cried.

Twenty-four hours later, she was still in Woodstock, and Malcolm was in the southern hemisphere.

Malcolm shook himself out of his memories and hit the gas, speeding away from Woody's bar and running the last light before finally leaving town, heading into the blackness that swallowed Route 11. There was nowhere else to go. He was two miles from his sister, his brother, and a reunion with history.

Once again the scent of Rain's perfume blew past him.

CHAPTER 8

Malcolm took the left off the highway and drove up the familiar driveway that led to *Domus Jefferson* standing at the top of its grand hill. As the car rolled to a stop, his headlights revealed the Inn's customary quiet. It never seemed to matter how many people were staying or how much collective noise they produced, the Inn was always a scene from a watercolor picture book. Even in the visual chaos of ambulance lights and police cars and mourners on the day Jack and Laurel left, the air on that hill had been undeniably calm. Jack called the Inn's serenity *the spirit of Jefferson.* Malcolm called it *spooky.*

Malcolm counted just four cars: a 1979 Chevy El Camino, a Woodstock police cruiser, his mother's Volvo, and his father's green Chevy pickup. Malcolm killed the headlights and sat. On the darkened porch he pictured his mother embracing a skinny young man in a powder-blue tuxedo. Next to him stood his giddy, seventeen-year-old prom date. He stepped away from his mother and grabbed his date's hand, pretending not to see his father's out-stretched arms. "Be safe," he heard his mother call from behind him as he guided his date into the white limousine. Malcolm couldn't recall whether he answered or not. He only remembered the scent of Rain Jesperson's perfume on her neck as they danced under the chandelier at the Marriott in nearby Harrisonburg.

He pushed open the door of his rental and stepped out into the comfortable Woodstock evening. He grabbed his canvas duffle bag from the trunk and walked toward the Inn, the only sound coming from his heavy sandals grinding the fine gravel of the driveway. He climbed the six steps that led to the Inn's generous, renowned porch, the image from the front of *Domus Jefferson's* brochure.

"Hi, Malcolm," a voice said from the dark.

Malcolm jumped. "Hello?" He dropped his bag and turned to see two men—pastors—rocking in two of the six white rocking chairs that lined the porch and faced out into the night.

"Sorry, thought you saw us," said one of them as he stood.

"Geez, what made you think that? You scared the shi—"

"Malcolm!" the pastor said, familiar disapproval draping his voice.

"Sorry, Pastor B."

"It's good to see you. And you remember Pastor Doug White."

"Sure. Hi there, Pastor."

Pastor Doug stood and shook Malcolm's hand.

Pastor Doug and Pastor Braithwaite were the same height and approximately the same age. Pastor Braithwaite's hair was well groomed and hadn't appeared to grow or thin since the day Malcolm had first met him as a youngster attending church, often against his will. The pastor's hair was always perfectly trimmed over his ears and his bangs were plastered against his shiny forehead. He wore his customary white shirt, blue tie, and matching blue sport coat.

Pastor Doug, on the other hand, was frequently disheveled and tonight was no different. He had rapidly thinning hair on top of his head and long, uneven sideburns. He wore a black windbreaker over a white shirt and a loosely-knotted black knit tie. His black polyester pants were too snug and light brown socks led to black tennis shoes with black laces.

When Malcolm shook Pastor Doug's hand, his fingers brushed past the remains of a scar on his wrist. Malcolm had always wanted to ask. He never had.

The two pastors had been inseparable, at least in Malcolm's eyes, for a decade. Pastor Doug served in a small church off Route 7 in Winchester and from time-to-time made his way through the Valley with Pastor Braithwaite always dutifully at his side.

"I got the call from A&P," Pastor Braithwaite said. "We're so sorry, Malcolm. We're here to help."

Malcolm nodded and in his peripheral vision saw his sister approach the Inn's open front door.

"I guess I thought I might find someone waiting for me," he continued, raising his voice, "but I expected it to be one of the town pigs."

"Malcolm!" The shout came from inside the screen door. "Don't talk about your sister like that!" Samantha flew through the door and ran toward her brother, catapulting into his chest, knocking him backward and nearly back down the stairs.

"Eeeeasy girl!" he said. "I knew you were sneaking around here somewhere." He flexed every muscle in his arms and legs to keep the teetering twosome from falling down. "It's not like I haven't seen you in two years."

Samantha let go and punched her brother in the chest. "Actually, Dip Stick, it *is* like you haven't seen me in two years."

"Has it been that long? Really? It seems only yesterday since you last called me that."

"You'll hear more than that before this night ends."

"Can't wait . . . Speaking of which, where's my niece?"

"At the Godfrey's. She's been there since I told her the news. I didn't want Angela to be at our place alone."

"You tell Angie her favorite uncle is in town. That will cheer her up."

"She knows—he took her out for ice cream this afternoon." Samantha laughed before she'd even finished the joke.

"Well now, we better let you children catch up," Pastor Braithwaite interrupted, bending down to grab his brown leather briefcase. "We ought to get home anyway. Pastor Doug's staying with my family for a few days."

"That's sweet of you, Pastor," Samantha offered.

Pastor Braithwaite stepped down the stairs and Pastor Doug followed, pausing briefly as he passed Malcolm. "It's good to see you, kids. And I'm sorry about your mother and father." He put one hand on Malcolm's shoulder and looked him in the eye.

"Thanks, Pastor."

"If you need to talk, any of you, just call Pastor Braithwaite's."

"That's sweet. Thanks you two," Samantha said loudly enough for Braithwaite to hear.

Pastor Doug descended the stairs in slow, lanky, and deliberate steps. He stopped at the bottom to offer an awkward wave with a long, thin arm, before ducking into Pastor Braithwaite's car. Seconds later the car rolled slowly down the long driveway and into the darkness.

"Strange ducks, eh?" Malcolm said, turning back to Samantha.

"Shut it and hug me again." Samantha pulled him close, hugging him tight and breathing in the lingering smell of river water from his unruly beard. "I don't know what's worse, Mal, Mom and Dad being gone or the heinous smell you're shooting off. When did you last shower?"

"Couple days ago, and it was more of a bath; and it wasn't in water so much as a mud hole."

"Brazil?"

"Brazil."

"Well, I don't care what you smell like, I'm glad you're here." She tightened her grip on him. "I missed you, Mal."

"I'm easy to miss, Sammie."

She lifted her head off his shoulder. "I'm serious. You don't prepare for this. I've known death could take Dad on a whim for a while now. But Mom?" She buried her head in his chest and began to cry.

"Come on, now, now, let's go in." He picked up his bag and followed his sister into the house. He stopped for a moment in the foyer to survey the quiet house. "Matt around?"

"He's over visiting Rosie and Rick Schwartz in Mount Jackson, but he'll be back. He's staying here." Sam blew her nose.

"The Schwartzes are still alive?" Malcolm asked.

"Come on, Mal, you haven't been gone that long. Rick's still got his clinic and Rosie's still mayor, going on ten years now."

"I guess nothing much changes around here, does it." It wasn't a question.

"No," Samantha answered anyway. "Woodstock is always Woodstock and the Coopers are always the Coopers. That's what Dad said anyway."

Malcolm dropped his bag at the bottom of the stairs and walked down the long corridor toward the kitchen. He stopped halfway to straighten a slightly crooked frame holding an aged penny.

"The Inn smells different."

"That's because no one's been cooking." Samantha sat at the lengthy dining room table. Malcolm sat across from her. The eggshell-white walls were lined with pictures of war heroes and presidents. Expensive china was displayed behind the glass doors of an antique, handmade cabinet Jack had purchased at an auction in Waynesboro the year they moved to Woodstock. An architect's rendering of Monticello hung on the opposite wall between pictures of Jefferson and Washington. Behind Malcolm hung a painting of Washington praying in the snow at Valley Forge. It was one of Jack's favorite pieces of art.

"Remember the smells of Mom's breakfasts?" Samantha leaned her elbows on the table. "That French toast she made? Soaking fat pieces of Texas toast in her syrup batter all night? And the Virginia ham. The smells were so good they lasted until dinner."

"Mom could cook, couldn't she." Malcolm rested his hands behind his head, intertwining his fingers, and staring up at the ceiling.

"It's what she did best," Samantha answered. "I wish I'd eaten here more the last couple of years."

The two sat quietly, gazing at the family portraits and antique artwork that lined the walls. Eventually Samantha rested her head on her folded arms atop the table. She gazed up at her brother and admired Malcolm's rugged features. She noted that even road weary with a long, mangy beard, he was a handsome man.

"When's the funeral?" Malcolm asked.

"Sunday night at the church. Viewing is Saturday."

"A Sunday funeral?"

"Dad's request. He told the church, made them promise. I think he even wrote it in the paperwork when he pre-paid."

"He pre-paid? That's so—so—"

"So Dad?"

"Yep."

"And the viewing is at the church, too?"

"No, it's at the Guthrie Funeral Home in Edinburg."

"Ariek Guthrie is still alive?"

"Malcolm."

"Sorry, Sis, old jokes die hard."

Samantha snickered and the two fell quiet again.

"She's actually at Guthrie's right now, in case you wondered," Samantha said several minutes later.

"Where?"

"Guthrie's."

"Who?"

"Nancy Reagan, who do you think?"

"Cool. What's the Nanster doing in town?"

"You're such a doof. You know who."

Malcolm leaned back in his chair and looked up. "Rain."

"She asked about you, you know."

"She's still alive, too?"

"Malcolm. Stop."

"Stop what? I'm not sure what to say here, Sam."

"Don't you want to know how she is?"

"Not really."

"Liar."

"Fine, how is she?"

"Miserable."

"Right."

Samantha winked. "And single." Malcolm sat up.

"The wedding's been put off three times now. The first time was legit, though. Rain's aunt up in Gaithersburg had surgery and needed some help for a few months, so Rain drove up there and stayed with her. Nathan said he was fine about it, but I could tell it really irritated him."

"Which you must have thoroughly enjoyed," Malcolm smiled.

Samantha's lips smiled but she said nothing.

"I can't believe it. I just assumed it'd happened."

"Well, you haven't exactly been the easiest guy to track down. I've tried calling that dumb phone Mom bought you at least fifty times."

"I didn't turn it on much, I guess. It's lucky you caught me Thursday."

"So where were you?"

"On a boat on the Amazon, up north in Manaus, taking pictures and writing."

"Writing?"

"My book, remember?"

"That was two years ago, Mal. I thought you'd be finished by now."

"Me too. I caught a nasty case of writer's block down there."

"Better than worms," Samantha smiled.

"Got those too," Malcolm deadpanned.

Samantha feigned beating her head against the table. They laughed together like two people reliving a twenty-year-old inside joke.

"So when do we talk about it?" Samantha asked when the laughter faded to only periodic giggles.

"Here it comes."

"Can't ignore the elephant forever."

"Truthfully, I'm surprised you lasted this long."

"This isn't easy, Malcolm."

"I'm serious. I thought Nathan or one of his boys would be waiting."

"He and Matt worked something out. You have a couple of days, but after the funeral we'll have to deal with it."

"Matt made a deal with Nathan to keep him out of my face? That couldn't have been easy."

"It wasn't. But it's done. And Matt really went the distance for you."

"What's the catch? You going to hold my hand for three days?"

"Not quite, but I need your keys."

"What?"

"Your keys, Mal."

"You've got to be kidding."

"I'm not. No driving. Your license is suspended."

"What?"

"It's standard procedure. They revoke your license when someone with a record like yours decides to skip town on bail, imagine that."

"Come on, Sis, I'll be good."

"Sorry, Mal, this is my job—*my job*—on the line."

Malcolm pulled the keys from a pocket on his baggy camping shorts and slid them across the table.

"Sorry." Samantha closed her hand around the keys.

"I know. And I'm sorry you have to babysit."

"Don't be sorry, at least not about that." Samantha reached across and took Malcolm's hand. "You did the right thing."

"Did I?"

"Yes. You didn't have to come back."

"Mom and Dad are dead. How could I *not* come back?"

"Even still, I'm proud of you. Mom and Dad would be, too."

"Let's see if you still feel that way Sunday night."

"No trouble, Mal. Please?"

"Cross my heart, hope to die," Malcolm said, crossing his chest with his index finger.

"I love you, Doof."

CHAPTER 9

S amantha led Malcolm upstairs and described the scene A&P reported when she pushed the door open Thursday morning to find Jack and Laurel lying dead in one another's arms. Samantha explained that their mother had been tormented by the fact that Malcolm hadn't known their father was dying of cancer.

"It ate at her, Mal."

"I'm sorry for her, but Dad and I hadn't had a real conversation for two or three years before I left. Can't say I would have rushed home if I'd known."

"He's our father, Mal, *your father. Your blood.*" She let the words hit him. "You would have come."

"Probably," he nodded, though he still doubted.

Samantha carefully shared the coroner's best-guess on how and why their parents had died two nights earlier. She reminded Malcolm that their family had a history of heart disease and though Laurel had never felt at-risk of a heart attack, her occasional heartburn was now proven to have been more than a mere inconvenience.

"You know Mom," Samantha said, taking a seat on the foot of the bed. "She just never stopped. You remember the summer she broke her ankle at Lake Caroline but said it was just a sprain? She walked on that fracture for two weeks before Dad made her go in—"

"Yeah, yeah, and Dad was mad," Malcolm cut in. "Oh jeez, he was mad. Then the doc put the X-ray up. 'See, Laurel,'" Malcolm mimicked his father's low, authoritative voice. "'It's a frac-ture, dadblastit! It's—a—frac-ture! I told you it was a frac-ture.'"

"Be nice," Samantha said, though she, too, laughed at the impersonation. "Mom could fight through anything."

"Except a heart attack," Malcolm said.

"Except a heart attack."

They moved from room to room. Malcolm noticed a few new pieces of art and a new canopy bed in one of the upstairs guest rooms. "Someone's honeymoon antics. Don't ask," Samantha grinned.

They ended up in the small library and Samantha began unloading two years of her personal history. She'd gotten a pay raise when the county tried to lure her from the town's police force to their own. The other job was more money, Samantha admitted, but working countywide meant more time away from her daughter and being much farther away from the Inn. She ran a greater chance of not being nearby if their parents needed something.

Malcolm asked about Will Armistead, Samantha's former high-school sweetheart and her ex-husband of six years. She explained that he'd recently moved from nearby Arlington down to Atlanta to work for a public relations firm.

"Do you miss him at all?" Malcolm asked.

"You know that itch when you get poison ivy in between your fingers? You scratch and you scratch, but the more you scratch, the more you know the itch is still there. Then you stop scratching and it slowly fades away in a week or two. By the third week, you remember the itch, but it feels better, you know?"

"I don't get it."

"Oh shut it, you do too. Well, it's taken six years, but it finally feels like three weeks. The rash is gone."

"So you really miss him then?"

"I know Ang misses him," Samantha said, "but she knows Atlanta isn't that far away. Maybe I'll fly her down for a visit this year." Samantha shrugged. "I'm slowly getting over the hard feelings. Maybe if he comes up for a visit, I'll buy him a drink at Woody's."

"And what about acting? You back at it yet?"

"No, not yet."

"Because . . . ?"

"Someday, Mal."

"When?"

"Someday. I don't know." She rested her head on her right hand. "With Mom and Dad lately . . . and now all this . . . There's just been no time." Her voice trailed off. "And Will took such pleasure in squashing those dreams."

"But not the talent."

"Who knows?"

"Get to it, Sis, it's about time. There's probably something happening in Harrisonburg. There's always some show at JMU."

"Maybe."

Malcolm winked at her.

"Thank you," she said.

As the moment settled between them the front door opened downstairs. "Hello?" Samantha called.

"It's just me," Matthew called out.

"We're up here," Samantha answered. "Be sweet," she whispered to Malcolm.

Seconds later, Matthew appeared. Though the double-Windsor knot on his power red tie was loosened slightly, he still wore the sport coat he'd been in all day.

"Malcolm, you made it," he said, extending his right hand.

Instead of shaking it, Malcolm stood and took it gently, and, after quickly licking his lips, kissed it.

"What's wrong with you?" Matthew shook his head and wiped his hand across his brother's shirt.

"Sammie told me to be sweet."

She rolled her eyes.

"Well, it's good to see you regardless," Matthew said. "Even though you look like trash."

"Why thank you. I actually wore your old Girl Scout uniform on the plane but changed when I got here—"

"Okay, boys, that's plenty. Let's try harder, shall we?"

"She's right," Matthew offered.

"Yes, she is," and Malcolm dutifully stretched out his hand. But when Matthew took it, Malcolm yanked it up and kissed it once again.

"Grow up already," Matthew barked, wiping his hand once again across his brother's chest, this time with force.

"Alrighty, downstairs, kids." Samantha took charge, as she'd done many times before, and shoved both men out the door and down the stairs. "And let's not forget," she called, trailing behind them, "I'm armed."

The three siblings gathered in the spacious living room. Malcolm sprawled out on one of the two leather couches, Matthew finally removed his jacket and settled into a recliner, and Samantha sat on the stone hearth that guarded the fireplace. The evening's once-warm fire had faded into cool dancing flickers from the remains of two stubborn logs.

"Uncle Joe coming?" Malcolm asked.

"Not sure he's gotten the word yet."

"You know he wrote me once when I lived in Sete Lagoas—probably been a year at least—said he was sober, moving to St. Louis for work, met some lady."

"That's true," Samantha answered. "He has been doing better. Dad said Joe's been sober for three years, maybe more."

"So *he* says," Matthew added.

"So his new *parole officer* says," said Samantha firmly.

Matthew nodded a half-hearted apology. "Well, I hope he makes it. Would be nice to see him. Maybe he can tell me what to expect in the pokey," Malcolm grinned.

"Moving on . . ." Samantha prodded.

"So, Matt, Sammie here tells me I'm grounded for a few days," Malcolm said, ignoring Samantha and wrapping his arms around the throw pillow on the couch.

"You could put it that way," Matthew replied.

"And then what? What happens Monday morning?"

"We sit down with Nathan and a couple guys from the county and they arrest you quietly."

"And then?"

"Then it's up to Judge Houston."

"Come on, Matthew, you don't have any idea what they're thinking?"

"They're thinking you were already on probation for what—three fights in a year? Plus you destroyed that guy's motorcycle."

"Your point?"

"Then you assaulted that guy at Woody's and went *way, way* too far. You almost killed him."

"Almost," Malcolm said.

"Whatever, you almost killed the guy. And you punched Nathan Crescimanno for good measure."

"Twice," Malcolm said with a grin.

"Exactly."

"He deserved it."

"Oh, I'm sure. But let's not forget you ran on your bail. No, wait, no, you ran on *Dad's* bail, the bail *Dad* paid to keep you out of jail for all your previous . . . indiscretions," Matthew's lip curled and he shook his head.

"Two words, Matthew: Self. Defense."

"Self-defense? Come on. If you believed that, why did you run? Why did you hide?"

Because Brazil was a lot more scenic than prison, Malcolm thought. *And there was a lot less Rain.* Malcolm smiled ironically and looked away.

"Self-defense," Matthew mocked, gesturing quotes with his fingers. "You were afraid the guy was going to bite your ankles while you kicked his ribs for two minutes? And you broke Nathan's nose because he what? He stole your girlfriend?"

"Boys, *stop it,*" Samantha said.

Malcolm ignored her. "Maybe the guy had a gun."

"He didn't—"

"What if it had been Monica, huh, Matt? You would have shaken the guy's hand and walked away?"

"Monica's my wife, you idiot. Big difference!" Matthew couldn't remember the last time he'd raised his voice and he struggled to contain his anger. He hated how easily Malcolm could get under his skin.

From her spot across the room Samantha dropped her head into her hands. As the arguing ebbed and flowed around her, Samantha wished her parents would appear one last time to mediate. She hoped the rest of the weekend would pass in a blink. She prayed for strength. She regretted that Rain had been in the bar that night and that Malcolm had inherited his father's temper.

A fall Friday night in Woodstock meant high school football. The passion wasn't quite Texas-sized, but it was rich and genuine. Win or lose, it made no difference: the town loved their Falcons. You could count on one hand the number of people in Woodstock without some connection to the school or team.

That Friday night's game ended with a win: the visiting Strasburg Rams missed a field goal with four seconds left. The Falcons and many of their classmates celebrated with a pizza party in the school cafeteria. Their fathers celebrated with $1 beer at Woody's on Main Street.

Malcolm was in town visiting his parents for the weekend. Though he had an apartment thirty miles away in Front Royal, where he worked part-time for the Virginia Park Service, Malcolm spent nearly as much time eating at *Domus Jefferson* as he did in his own kitchen. He enjoyed his mother's cooking, but it was the scenery he appreciated the most. Rain had been managing the day-to-day affairs of the Inn for a couple of years. Though Rain broke Malcolm's heart shortly after he dropped out of college at James Madison University, their friendship had miraculously survived.

In Malcolm's spare time, he chased freelancing opportunities with *Rolling Stone, National Geographic, Time;* he'd even pitched *Redbook.* Even back then, he'd fancied himself a novelist, though he had only three published articles to his credit.

Malcolm wedged his Volkswagen Rabbit between a pickup and a Honda Accord. He was three blocks away from Woody's, nearly the entire distance from one end of historic downtown to the other. He walked in at 10:35 and immediately spotted Rain chatting with two girlfriends at the far end of the bar; his eyes were well-trained.

Though Rain had never been a drinker—in fact, Malcolm couldn't recall ever seeing her drink at all—she was a staple at any celebration. He knew by that hour of the night she was hauling half a dozen sets of car keys in her purse. She always said she just liked a good party and good friends, but Malcolm knew otherwise. Her father drove himself and a nearly empty bottle of vodka into a tree driving home from a seminar in Charleston in 1975.

Malcolm caught Rain's eye and smiled. He mouthed an

over-obvious hello from across the room, making his lips ten times bigger than necessary. She mouthed *hello* back in the same silly way. Then he complimented her recent haircut by creating finger scissors and pretending to cut his bangs. He added an exaggerated wink. She smiled wide and gave him the sign for *thank you*: sliding her hand along her chin, exposing her soft palm. Before he could reply, his view was obscured by a sliding gaggle of patrons.

Malcolm made his rounds. He shook hands, hugged a few overly-friendly women he remembered from high school, and slapped energetic high-fives with the increasingly inebriated football crowd. He heard ten different play-by-play accounts of the final drive and the Falcon's brave defensive stand. One fan said the thirty-five-yard, game-determining field goal attempt sailed wide right. Another argued that the ball hit the left upright. "Who cares? It missed! WE WON!" added yet another, and the trio raised their drinks to the sky and went for another round.

Malcolm soaked in the sounds and the smells and imagined it might make for a nice feature in *Sports Illustrated:* "The Fans of Small Town Football." He liked the idea. He scribbled the title on a cocktail napkin and tucked it in his pocket.

As midnight approached, Malcolm became mindful of the shrinking distance between Rain and an unfamiliar man sporting a shiny bald spot and a tweed sport coat. "Tweed? Please," Malcolm scoffed loudly enough someone might have heard him if the decibel level in the bar hadn't been so high.

He surveyed the entire bar and wondered where Nathan Crescimanno was lurking. Nathan had been Rain's boyfriend for the past year or so. And though Rain and Malcolm didn't discuss it, he feared an engagement with Nathan was a looming possibility. The thought made him dizzy.

Nathan, for his part, had spent much of the past year letting anyone with ears know that marriage and kids with Rain was just step one. Nathan had it all planned out: Get married, have a boy and a girl in successive years, run for the House of Delegates, have another boy, serve two terms, have one more girl, run for Attorney General, and four years later run for his dream job as Governor of the Commonwealth of Virginia. He liked to think he was bred for it.

Malcolm agreed. No one could sling it like Nathan.

Nathan was the only man Rain had ever dated besides Malcolm. When Malcolm and Rain were dating, he'd refused to propose until he could afford a ring, a honeymoon, a house, children, *and* their college tuitions at Ivy League schools. Rain grew tired of waiting for one thing and he was tired of waiting for another. And though it became the primary reason for their breakup, Malcolm eventually learned to appreciate, even admire, her faithful chastity. Now it crushed Malcolm to know Nathan was poised to be the beneficiary of her purity.

Nathan was a good man, Malcolm reminded himself, even if

his unbridled ambition made the Cooper family nervous for the future of Virginia and her citizens.

Malcolm shook the thought from his head—it wasn't like Nathan to let Rain socialize this long without him at her side.

"Coop!" a drunk Lonnie Smallwood yelled, slapping Malcolm so hard on the back he nearly lost his breath. "Where ya been, man? Ain't seen ya 'round for a while."

"I've been here; you've just been drunk."

"Now don't go saying that," Lonnie slurred. "I'm usually sober on Mondays."

"Well that explains it—I work Mondays."

"Riiiight," Lonnie stammered. "You even allowed in here? Aren't you, like, on probation or something?"

Malcolm wasn't listening. His eyes went to Rain's stool at the bar, but it had been taken by someone in a black foam, ten-gallon cowboy hat. Rain's girlfriends were still at the bar, but they were trapped in conversations with grown men wearing grass-stained Washington Redskins football jerseys.

"Tweed," Malcolm said. The man in the sport coat—and Rain—were gone. "I gotta run, Lonnie," he said, turning quickly toward the door.

"Later, Coop, let's go huntin' sometime!"

Malcolm stepped out the front door and looked up and down Main Street. He took a few steps north and heard Tweed's voice coming from the alley.

"Come on, baby, I hear you're clean as snow." Tweed pulled on Rain's blouse.

"Get off, get off!" she growled, swatting at him with her hands.

Malcolm sprinted toward them and launched himself at the man, burying the point of his right shoulder into Tweed's chest and sending him flying into the air like a football dummy. Malcolm stood, towering over him, and with a single right hook, cracked his jaw so hard that the sound echoed between the Civil War-era brick buildings.

"Get up."

"Get lost," Tweed answered, spitting blood onto Malcolm's tennis shoe.

Malcolm turned to Rain. "Are you okay?" Before she answered, Malcolm quickly turned and kicked Tweed in the stomach with as much force as his leg had ever generated.

Tweed groaned and rolled to his other side, facing away from Malcolm.

Malcolm turned him on his back again and planted one foot firmly on his solar plexus.

"Rain!" a voice called from the corner. Nathan.

"Nate!" Rain ran toward him and he swallowed her in his arms.

"What happened?" he said, smoothing her hair and holding her close.

"This guy . . . That creep . . . He grabbed . . . Grabbed at me . . . Touched me . . . Pulled my top halfway off . . ."

"Shhh, you're safe now. Go get in my car, it's right across the street, see it? It's open." She resisted, gripping his arm so hard it left marks. "You're okay. *Go.*"

"Shouldn't you . . . shouldn't you call the station?" Rain continued struggling to find air.

"*Go get in the car. Now.*" He softened. "Rain, you're okay, I'll handle this."

She turned and ran.

Malcolm turned again to Tweed and kicked him high in the ribs. He broke two with his first strike.

"Whoa! That's enough, Malcolm." Nathan reached for his arm.

"Enough? Oh, you want your shot? Be my guest." Malcolm stepped aside and gestured at the man's stomach. "You're up."

"No, I mean that's *enough*. He gets the point."

"Yeah, I get it," the man labored, "and the girl's not worth it."

Malcolm kicked him again, harder than the first time, grunting when his foot made contact. When the man instinctively covered his torso, Malcolm took four more vicious shots at his face, the last a brutal uppercut that knocked him unconscious and sent a tooth loosened from a previous blow soaring from his mouth.

"Malcolm!" Nathan yelled. "*Enough!* He's right."

"What?" Malcolm turned to Nathan.

"She's not worth it."

Malcolm stared at him wide-eyed.

77

"We all know Rain's got more going on outside than inside."

"*What did you say?* Are you drunk? What is your problem?"

"I've got no problem. Just opportunities. And Rain's been giving *plenty* of them to me lately, if you know what I mean."

"*What?*"

"You need me to write you a memo? We got engaged last night. And the long cold winter is over."

Without a second thought, Malcolm drilled the Shenandoah County Commonwealth's Attorney squarely in the nose. Dark red blood dripped from both nostrils onto his lips. The swelling began on contact.

Nathan Crescimanno smiled through the pain.

Malcolm punched him one more time.

"You're mine," Nathan said, smiling. He spit blood on the sidewalk.

Without meaning to, Samantha had moved from the hearth to a soft bearskin rug in the middle of the living room and fallen asleep. She awoke after midnight to an empty room and the sound of a car screeching and spitting gravel onto Route 11. She wiped her eyes and stepped onto the porch. Matthew was sitting in a rocking chair.

"Who was that?" she asked, still groggy.

"Your brother."

"What?" she said, now very much awake.

"Your brother. He's cooling off."

"In whose car?"

Matthew didn't have to answer. Samantha's mouth dropped open.

Her police cruiser was gone.

CHAPTER 10

R ain spent the evening at home. She made tearful calls to friends and family of the Coopers. She relayed the very latest information on the schedule for the weekend.

Saturday afternoon the Cooper children were hosting a private lunch for some close friends and regular guests of *Domus Jefferson*. A&P was coordinating.

Saturday night, Jack and Laurel would be available for viewing at Guthrie's from six to eight P.M.

Sunday morning, A&P had arranged for a special choir tribute to be performed at the church in Mount Jackson. It was a kind gesture on the church's part, made easier by the promise of a generous donation from an anonymous donor. When things settled, A&P would mail a check to the church for $5,000. She was also funding a brunch Sunday afternoon for anyone coming in for the funeral from out-of-town. The Coopers were expecting a hundred guests, maybe more. Finally, late that afternoon, the funeral would be held at the same church, with Pastor Braithwaite presiding, and the interment would follow at Massanutten Cemetery.

Rain thought the calendar read more like Super Bowl week than a funeral.

Nathan made a few calls from his office on Lawyers' Row, a series of small offices near the courthouse. He paced. He reread Malcolm's file and police report—again. He called an old law school buddy. He paced. He admired an 11x17 portrait of Rain displayed below his diplomas and credentials on the wall across the room. He called the funeral home, woke Ariek Guthrie, and asked if the plans were going smoothly for the viewing and funeral on Sunday.

"Everything is in order, Mr. Crescimanno. Please don't call again; it's late." He sighed. "Listen, I'm sorry. Why don't you check in again Sunday afternoon? Fair enough?"

"Fair," Nathan responded, annoyed, and hung up without a good-bye.

Rain wore her favorite sweatpants and Washington Bullets basketball sweatshirt. She made lists, reviewed them, added names, and scratched through others. She hand-washed the clean dishes in the new Sears dishwasher Nathan had bought for her and paid to have installed.

The phone rang. It was Nathan—again. "I'm fine," she said—again. "Stop worrying, Nate. I'll see you tomorrow."

She pulled a 1974 Central High yearbook from underneath a stack of sweaters on a shelf in her closet. She flipped through the pages, surprised at how many people she now realized had moved from the Valley. The book fell open to a familiar, dog-eared page. Malcolm and Rain stood arm-in-arm beneath a giant Falcon piñata. He wore his father's powder-blue tuxedo. She wore anxiety and a pink dress.

Nathan called his bank at the 24-hour, toll-free number and checked his savings and money-market balances. He called his brother in Sacramento and got his answering machine. He didn't leave a message. He re-labeled a few of his files and reviewed the court docket for the upcoming week. He looked at Rain's picture on the wall again. He knelt by his $400 burgundy leather office chair and prayed for the first time in a decade. He prayed his dreams wouldn't unravel. He prayed that God would prompt his estranged father to eventually be proud of him. He begged that the only woman who'd ever understood him, ever loved him, wouldn't be swept back into the exotic life of Malcolm Cooper.

Rain also prayed for the fourth time that day, and slept alone.

CHAPTER 11

At 1:30 A.M. on Saturday morning, Matthew, Samantha, and A&P were sifting through boxes of paperwork at the dining room table when they heard a noise in the driveway and saw two sets of headlights illuminating the foyer. Samantha jumped from her seat and ran to the front door.

"You better stay," Matthew said to A&P as he stood to follow. "This will be ugly."

"Say no more. Castro and I will mind the store." After Matthew vanished down the hall, A&P picked the cat up from the floor and placed him on the table next to a pile of papers from a box. "Your hearing still good?"

Castro blinked twice.

Samantha charged down the porch stairs just as an officer opened the rear door of Samantha's cruiser.

Malcolm stepped out, handcuffed and angry. "Can you believe this, Sammie? They cuffed me!"

"Sorry, Malcolm," Keith said. "Your sister's orders."

"You don't have to apologize, Keith," Samantha said. "Malcolm, handcuffs are the least of your concerns right now. What were you thinking?"

She gestured at the cuffs and Keith quickly removed them.

"I'm a victim here, Sammie. It's police brutality! Everyone knows I bruise easily!"

"Shut it!" Samantha shrieked loud enough that back inside the Inn, A&P raised her eyebrows while Castro jumped off the table and scurried to safety underneath A&P's chair.

Samantha turned to the two officers. "So how bad is it? Where did you find him?"

"He was sitting outside the movie theater on Main."

"That's it?"

"Yeah," Malcolm answered for them. "I wanted to be first in line for *The Princess Bride.* I have a lot of movies to catch up on. Where's the crime in that?"

"The crime's the stolen car."

"Technicality."

She glared at Malcolm. Not pulling her eyes from him, she said to the officers, "I'm sorry, guys. This will *not* happen again."

"Don't worry," Keith smiled and tossed Samantha her keys.

"I appreciate that. And thanks for bringing my wheels back."

"Sure. 'Night, Sam. 'Night, Malcolm," Barry said, and then noticed Matthew standing on the porch. "Oh, hey, Matt."

"Hey, guys."

"Sorry about your folks."

"Thanks," Matthew said. "And thanks for bringing my kid brother back."

The two officers climbed into the second police car and drove away, free to laugh once they'd pulled onto Route 11. They did.

"Thanks, Sis. I was worried you'd be mad."

"Oh, I'm mad. I'm *more* than mad. I'm so ticked I could kick your butt from here back to Brazil."

"You know, that Keith guy is a real cat. I think he's sweet on you." Malcolm lowered his voice to sound extra sultry. "I could hear things in the car."

Matthew laughed from the front porch.

"Something funny, Matt?" she snapped over her shoulder, though her eyes remained trained on Malcolm.

"Hey y'all," A&P called through the screen door. "Come see what I found."

"We'll finish this later," Samantha said as Malcolm moved toward the steps and followed Matthew into the house. She held the door open and as Malcolm passed through, she smacked him hard on the back of the head with the hand that held her keys.

They gathered around the table. Malcolm gave A&P a hug, kissed her on the cheek and whispered, "Thank you, *for everything*" in her ear. She kissed him back.

"What'd you find, Anna Belle?" Samantha asked, still flustered.

"So I finished that last box, and I went back to the basement looking for the other boxes that had tax documents, the ones you asked for, Matthew, and I found this one." She pulled a box from the floor that was labeled *"LC '48-'55."* "They're letters. From your dad to your mom. At least that's all I see in this box."

"I always thought those boxes were tax returns or something," said Samantha.

Matthew was puzzled. "I don't think I've ever seen them before. Are there more?"

"Don't know. I opened this one downstairs and brought it right up. Look in the back, boys, past the food storage, against the wall. The writing faces away so they look like regular boxes, nothing special."

For fifteen minutes Samantha and A&P read while the brothers made trips to the basement, retrieving boxes and stacking them around the dining room table.

After a while, A&P gathered her purse and her cat, kissed each of the Coopers good-bye and walked toward the back door. "Look around that table, kids," she said, turning to pull the door shut behind her. "You're all you've got." She wanted to say more, but didn't. Instead she talked to Castro all the way home.

Some letters they read quietly to themselves and solemnly returned to their envelopes like bodies to their caskets. Others they shared with the group. Many of the letters were uninteresting recaps of weeks spent together and apart. Many had stamps with postmarks from Richmond, Charlottesville, Norfolk, New York, and Memphis. Some had never been mailed and the children imagined they'd been slid under Laurel's pillows or into her latest book. They thought a select few seemed too personal to be finished and were silently mixed back into the high stacks.

Jack's letters appeared on photocopy paper, lined notebook paper, tattered spiral notebook paper, and hotel stationery. Several were even scribbled on napkins. Matthew found one stapled to a dollar bill and another written on the back of a flier announcing celebrity appearances at a special advance screening in Washington, D.C., of *Star Trek: The Motion Picture.*

November 14, 1979
Laurel,

It's Wednesday, but just barely! I'm sitting in the parking lot of the theater and all I've got to write on is a flier from tonight. I'm watching Joe tell jokes to some women across the street.

But time for the news of the night. You better be sitting. I MET WILLIAM SHATNER!

Did you hear that? I MET WILLIAM SHATNER!

I was sure when they said there would be cast members from the show at the theater tonight they meant George Takei or some extra whose name you never knew. But as Joe and I were standing around the lobby, he just walked in. What a sight! He's just as nice in person as I thought he'd be. Some think he's a windbag and maybe he is. I think he's always in character. And really, who isn't?

I wish I'd thought to have him sign something. I was so nervous when he shook my hand that all I could say was, "Live long and prosper." He looked at me and just smiled. He didn't say I was the most pitiful sixty-two-year-old man he'd ever met, but I had to be. Probably had no idea what to say to me. Who cares? I MET WILLIAM SHATNER!

By the way, the movie was amazing! I can't wait to take the boys on opening night. You'll come with us, right?

You know what? Joe was really grateful for the night out, Laurel. He wanted me to thank you. And thanks from me too for being so great about it. He needed it.

By the time you read this I will have told you all this already, probably more than once, knowing me. Who cares? I love you.

And are you still sitting down? I love you more than Star Trek.

Jack (Kirk)

November 3, 1948
Laurel,

I don't have long. It's lunch and all the boys can talk about is the election. Someone said one of the papers even had a headline that said *"Dewey Defeats Truman!"* I would love to get my hands on that for the collection.

I wonder what would have happened if the Republicans had let MacArthur run instead. I would have been more excited about voting, for sure. Still, I thought Dewey had it won. That silly train tour or whistle tour or whatever President Truman called it must have worked.

So here it comes. Brace yourself. *YOU WERE RIGHT!* And now we all get to suffer through four more years of a Democrat. I hope you're happy, Laurel Cooper. You win!

No matter. I still love you. Be you a Democrat, Republican— even Dixiecrat. (By the way, Joe told me he was voting for Strom Thurmond, even if he was the only one. Maybe if he'd stuck with Dewey, I wouldn't be wearing black today.)

Love you,

Jack

P.S. I'm a man of my word. Here's your $1. I guess the buck stops here after all.

April 22, 1970

To my *"exquisite bride,"*

What a trip! More than any letter I've written so far, I am writing this one as if years from now, when I am dead and gone, you will find this and need it to remember the details of this amazing week. And because you'll be old and tired and ready to meet me in *heaven, you'll rely on these letters to fill in the holes from our years together. Maybe me leaving before you will cause you to lose your mind? To go crazy? Wishful thinking? I thought so.*

I can count on one hand the number of experiences I've ever had that will live in my mind until they drag me from this earth. If I'm lucky, I'll get to take this one with me.

Last night, against all odds, we visited Graceland! No, we didn't just "visit" Graceland, did we, dear? Last night was our second in Memphis. You'd been begging me for years to visit and, at last, we had dinner on Beale Street. It's a trip I wouldn't have dreamt of even a few months ago. But when the stars align you don't argue with them.

So tell me, Laurel Cooper, how and when did you become so convincing an actress? You had the King eating out of your hand! Who could have guessed it would go so well? Better than we planned?

I'll admit I'm still a little sore we didn't get a photo, but I understand their reasons. Can you imagine what would happen if we broke our promise and began telling people we got in to Graceland? That we met Elvis and Priscilla Presley? You were amazing. And, by the way, Elvis Presley made a pinkie promise with us. I bet that doesn't happen everyday.

It started at the security gate. You were divine. If I hadn't known you were fibbing, I would have broken into tears myself! You looked at that guard with such conviction and said you were thirty-six hours from certain death. "From what?" he laughed.

How did you keep a straight face when you told him you suffered from Asian Stone Lung Disorder? And your cough—your cough was brilliant! It sounded like you had marbles in your chest. I don't want to know when you found time to perfect that.

So he called into the house and got Priscilla on the phone. A miracle by itself, eh? When she asked him to escort us to the east entrance I thought I'd wet my pants. You took his hand and thanked him, and then while his mouth hung open, you kissed the back of his hand like it was the last thing you'd ever do in this life.

I bet you $1 that after he returned to his guard shack, he soaked his hand in rubbing alcohol for an hour.

Priscilla was so kind. So beautiful. She was also more gentle than I thought she'd be. What a true lady.

The tour was a bonus; I never imagined we'd see so much of the house. I would have liked to see upstairs, but I'm not sure my heart could have handled that much excitement.

After fifteen minutes, maybe a few more, as we stood at the door waiting for the guard to retrieve us, three cars pulled up. It couldn't have been more obvious who was in them if there had been a giant sign on top of the hood.

When the King got out and sauntered past us to kiss his wife, I swear you almost melted. She introduced us, explained why we were there and how close you were to death. His voice is still ringing—no singing—inside my head.

"You drove all the way to Memphis to meet us right as you're readyin' to meet your God?"

They should have handed you the Academy Award right then.

"It's always been my dream, Sir, to meet you and your"—cough cough—"exquisite bride."

And Samantha thinks she's the best actress in the family?

"Bless you, woman. God bless your soul." He hugged you and kissed your cheek and you about buckled again. I wonder what he would have done if I'd popped him in the chin.

While the guard came up to escort us back off the property, Elvis asked one of his boys to remove the license plate from one of his cars. He did, and he brought it over to us. Upon the King's request, the same man pulled a pen from his coat pocket and both the King and Priscilla signed the back.

What a trip!

I don't remember much else about the last few days in Tennessee. What's to remember besides our fifteen minutes with the King of Rock and Roll and his "exquisite" bride?

I can't wait for the kids to hear this story. I suppose one day when we're gone, they'll find this letter and suddenly realize why there's a Tennessee license plate on our bedroom wall.

> *I love you,*
> *Jack Cooper*
> *husband of the only known*
> *survivor of the Asian Stone*
> *Lung Disorder*

P.S. I think when we get home and the license plate is in a safe place we should send a letter and apologize. What do you think?

Before Samantha finished the P.S., Malcolm and Matthew pushed their chairs from the table and raced one another from the room and up the stairs, jostling for position and shoving one another into the walls. As they neared the door to the master bedroom, Matthew slowed down enough to let Malcolm sneak by and through the doorway. Then from behind Matthew shoved his brother onto the master bed and lunged for the Tennessee license plate hanging on the wall.

"I can't believe it!"

"What's it say?" Malcolm asked, rolling off the side of the bed, regaining his balance, and snatching the plate from his brother.

"'To Laurel and Jack,'" Malcolm read. "'Enjoy your last days. Elvis and Priscilla, 1970.'"

"Mom and Dad said this was a souvenir from their trip, not an autograph. I can't believe we didn't ever see this!"

"What a trip," Malcolm said, shaking his head. "What a trip."

The boys returned to the dining room to find Samantha crying.

"Sis, what's wrong? What'd you find?" Matthew asked.

She held up a letter. "Dad was asking Mom what she thought would happen to the Inn when he was gone."

Matthew and Malcolm sat.

"When was it written?" Matthew asked.

She looked at the date. "Last year, June."

"Think he knew?" Malcolm asked.

Samantha didn't answer.

"Dad and I actually talked about this over the holidays," Matthew said. "He told me Alex Palmer—"

"Who?" Malcolm interrupted.

"Dad's attorney. He's in Front Royal. Dad said Alex helped him update his will last year, I imagine after things got really bad for him. He and Mom have some money hidden away in a couple of accounts. Not a lot. Most of it went into this place. Dad had an insurance policy so Mom would be all right when he died." Matthew hesitated. "Anyway, there's some work to be done. I'll get with the attorney."

"Dad couldn't have imagined they'd be leaving us at the same time," Samantha mused.

No one spoke.

"And the Inn?" Malcolm eventually asked.

"We're supposed to split everything three ways, including the Inn. It will take a while to sell, though, they usually do. Unless . . ." Matthew looked at his sister across the table. "Unless one of us wants to run it. Dad made it clear that was his first choice."

Samantha and Malcolm stared at their brother.

"You know I can't," Matthew answered their looks. "I can't leave Boston. I've got clients, interests. And you know Monica's not going to live in Woodstock."

Samantha and Malcolm both nodded.

"I could. I guess." Samantha tried to smile.

"You're a cop," Malcolm said. "Your heart isn't in running a bed-and-breakfast."

Samantha knew he was right.

"What about keeping it anyway?" Malcolm asked. "Rain could run it."

"Maybe for a little while, Mal, but she'll be gone soon. No way Nathan stays in Woodstock for very long." Samantha regretted saying what they already knew. "Sorry." She rubbed Malcolm's forearm.

He smiled. "Forget it." He squeezed her hand. "Let's read."

CHAPTER 12

N o way!" Samantha said. "I found one from their wedding night, June 16, 1948." She unfolded it and held it for her brothers to examine.

"No, no, no!" Malcolm called out, playfully plugging his ears. "I don't want to hear any of that, put it away, put it away!"

"Oh, shut it, there's nothing like that in here. Dad was a gentleman."

"But are we sure we should be reading these at all?" Malcolm asked in an unusually serious tone, though he'd already read seven or eight from a collection he'd assembled before him.

"Mom wouldn't have saved them if she didn't want them to be read," Samantha retorted.

"She's right," Matthew joined in. "They had to know we'd find them. I just can't believe we never knew Dad was writing them."

"I saw him writing all the time," Samantha said, "but I thought it was work stuff. I'd ask him what he was working on and he'd say lists for work, or church notes, or his personal journal. But I never guessed it was letters to Mom. She never said a peep."

"Maybe because we weren't *supposed* to know." Malcolm stopped reading again. "Maybe we should wait. It doesn't feel right. They're not even buried yet."

"You wait all you like," Samantha said. "I'm reading."

June 16, 1948

Dear Mrs. Cooper,

Can you believe we're married? We're married! What a day. It's 11:50 and you're sound asleep across the room. Did you know angels snore? They do. At least you do. It's the funniest thing. Who knew women snored? You'll hate me for writing that, but what can you do? We're married!

I made a promise today at the church and I'm making another promise tonight. I'm going to write to you every week. No matter whether we're across America from each other or in the same room, I'm going to write to you. I thought about keeping a journal, but I don't think I'd be able to keep it up. And who would care? Letters, though. Letters will last.

I don't think I could say this to you if you were awake right now, but I think I can say it now: Thank you. Thank you for waiting. Thank you for making me wait. Tonight was just like I imagined. No. It was BETTER than I imagined. It was magic.

Now I'll make one more promise. (Can you believe it? I've never made so many promises in my life.) Laurel, I will always stand by you. No matter what. We're in everything together. No secrets. No surprises. And I will always be true. In every way.

I love you, Mrs. Jack Cooper.

$$JC$$

P.S. Sorry about my brother. We'll get him back at his wedding.

✉

Samantha folded the letter and slid it back into its envelope.

Malcolm and Matthew stared at each other from across the table.

"Unbelievable," Matthew said.

"Unbelievable," Malcolm repeated. It seemed to be all anyone could come up with.

Samantha pulled out another letter from the box and began reading. Malcolm and Matthew went back to their own letters.

For an hour the children passed letters around the table. Samantha cried the most, at almost every letter, but even her thick-skinned and thick-headed brothers teared up a time or two. "Okay, guys," she finally said. "One more each and we've got to get to bed. We've got a long day tomorrow and these aren't going anywhere." They each shuffled through one of the dusty boxes and pulled a final letter.

November 27, 1957

Dear Laurel,

I wish I knew why it's taken me so long to learn such simple words.

I am sorry.

I forget sometimes how dangerous my short Chicago fuse can be. Would you have ever guessed a good Christian girl like you would fall for a Cubs fan from the north side?

I'm tempted to make excuses for myself, but what excuse is there for barking at the woman I swore to love and cherish. That's not a question. There is no excuse.

We both know money is tight. At least on that we agree. And honestly, that might not change for much of our marriage.

I'm sorry you didn't marry an Ivy League man or a Rockefeller. You deserve that. You deserve better. I just wish you didn't have to work. At least not now.

Somehow we'll make it. We will. Do you trust me?

So, yes, I am sorry. I'm sorry for not yet being the man I promised to be.

Please don't give up on me.

Jack

Just two paragraphs into his, Matthew nudged Samantha. "Trade me," he whispered.

April 9, 1975
Laurel,

New York is greener than I expected. Of course there are plenty of sights and smells that I wouldn't want to bring home, but there are surprising flashes of green all around the city, even some whites here and there in the planter boxes and parks. I'd like to share it with you someday if I could.

I'm settled at a motel about six blocks from your Aunt Beverly's. Sammie looks good. I saw her and Bev walking through Times Square this afternoon. I wanted to run up and hug her and throttle her and hug her some more. But I didn't. Obviously. Del says I should back off another week at least. Give her time to miss home. It's hard when I miss her more than she misses me. Maybe that's not true?

(I forgot to tell you on the phone—I left my umbrella on the train. I bought another one up here. I'll check when I get back to D.C. to see if someone turned it in. Who knows? It ain't much of an umbrella.)

Tomorrow first thing I'm going by a theater to look for a man named E.B. Arthur. There is no way that boy's mother named him E.B. Maybe I'll ask.

Bev says the theater is called "Curtains." How about that? It's what they call off-off-off Broadway. I think that means it's so far off Broadway you have to take a cab to get to the real deal.

Bev's worried, but she's going to stick to the plan. Tonight she'll tell Sammie she heard that "Curtains" is holding auditions for up-and-comers. If this E.B. fellow has a conscience we're in trouble. But we're in the Big Apple and with theater types I don't think that will be a problem. I'll bet you a couple hundred dollars will do the trick. Let's hope. That's all I got. (Plus a new umbrella!)

Pray.

JC

"Dad followed you?" Samantha's brothers said in unison.

Samantha couldn't speak.

"Crap, crap, *triple* crap!" Malcolm punched each word louder than the next. "Matt, which box did that come from?"

"Wait, Malcolm," Samantha protested, "I don't know that I want—"

"Oh, yes, you do," Malcolm said. He quickly shuffled through a pile of letters until he found one marked April 16, 1975, in pencil on the outside of the yellowed envelope.

"Then let me," Samantha said, taking the letter from her brother and opening it carefully.

April 16, 1975
Dear LC,

   DATE LINE: NEW YORK CITY, NEW YORK, USA
   I have no idea if that's how they write it. But who cares. I know we spoke on the phone tonight, but collect calls can't match a Wednesday Letter, now can they, Hon?
   Tonight was the night. She had four lines and I bet I got them memorized faster than she did. It helps that I got an extra copy of the script from E.B. Arthur. (That cost me $35!) Plus I've been watching every rehearsal from upstairs. (Another $50!)
   I met Bev today at a diner around the corner from the theater while Samantha was in dress rehearsal. She says Samantha's been making Del practice the scene with her over and over.
   Laurel, our Sammie was a vision tonight. The play isn't much, trust me, but Sammie sure makes it something special. She came on stage just after the second intermission. Before she came out, my heart was beating so hard I swear someone could have heard. But when she walked on stage? My heart about stopped. She walked through the front door like she owned the place. Here was her big debut scene.

   MELINDA: (that's our Samantha)
   "I'm here to clean the carpets."

   MR. BURNS: (he's a gangster type)
   "They don't need cleanin'. Get lost."

MELINDA:

"Someone thinks they do, Sir. I have a work order."

MR. BURNS:

"Let me see it."

MELINDA:

"I must have left it downstairs. Let me go get it."

MR. BURNS:

"I don't know who you are, lady, but my carpets don't need cleaning. Now don't make me say it again."

Then Sammie, I mean Melinda, pulls a fake gun from her fake supply bag and shoots him in the chest five times!!!!!

MELINDA:

"They do now."

I don't know how they did it, but when the guy fell, he grabbed his chest and somehow they made blood come through his suit jacket. His whole chest was soaked red. I tell you, Laurel, the theater went nuts! The crowd laughed and cheered and laughed some more.

There weren't but seventy, maybe eighty people there, but they cheered our girl like she was Audrey Hepburn. As gorgeous as Sam looked tonight, she could have been.

Honest? I'm still angry she ran away. I'm angry I'm missing work and risking my job to spend $39 a night to sleep with cockroaches at *that motel. I'm sad it will be years before she knows I was here tonight, maybe even decades if we're lucky.*

I'm especially sad you and the boys weren't here. I'm sad because I know how much she'll fight me when I show up at Del and Bev's to drag her home in a few days.

But seeing her on that stage tonight made me realize something: She won't win an Oscar tonight, or whatever they give for plays, but our Samantha is a star. I've never loved that girl more.

Thanks for supporting my little scheme. Most wives wouldn't. (What am I saying here—NO other wife would!)

It's Wednesday. See you soon.

Miss you.

Jack

P.S. Spread the news: Our Sammie is an off-off-off Broadway star!

"Can I say it again?" Malcolm asked as Samantha blew her nose.

"What?" she sniffled.

"Crap!" he blurted much too loudly for the middle of the night. "Did you know any of that, Sis?"

"No." She shook her head numbly. "I don't even know what to say . . ."

"Let's recap," Malcolm said.

Matthew raised his finger as if to pause a tape recorder. "Allow me. Sam, Dad followed you. He arranged the whole thing and he stayed in a motel for what, two weeks? How could you not know?"

"How could *you* not know?" she fired back.

"I wasn't even living at home. I was almost finished with my grad work in Blacksburg." Matthew swiveled toward his brother. "What's *your* excuse?"

Malcolm shrugged. "I just remember Sam running away to New York when she was seventeen and a couple days later Dad went to some B&B maintenance convention in Chicago. I remember Mom asking me to help around the place while he was gone. Even paid me."

Matthew looked incredulous. "Maintenance convention? You're unreal."

"Guys," Samantha ended the scuffle before it began. "You're missing the point. Dad *paid* for me to be in that show. He *paid* for me. I only got the part because he *paid* for it."

"Yeah, Sam," Malcolm said with more tenderness than his tongue was accustomed to. "He paid. Then he let you stay in New York with Mom's aunt, someone you barely knew—jeez, it was someone *Mom* barely knew. Dad let you run around Broadway for two weeks before he showed up and acted like he didn't know anything."

"Yes, but he was always watching."

"Yeah, that's right, he was always watching." Malcolm's voice trailed off and he began flipping through another stack. Samantha folded the letter, returned it to its envelope, and tucked it in the pocket of her polyester blue shirt, right beneath her golden Woodstock police badge.

CHAPTER 13

Saturday Morning

Malcolm and Matthew slept until almost 9:00 A.M. Only Samantha's tickling them under their necks in their respective beds kept them from sleeping until noon.

"Go away," Malcolm said, protecting his head under a pillow. "It's early."

"Wrong, it's *late*." She pulled the comforter off him and put her hand over her mouth and nose. "You're showering. Now. The whole Inn smells like a sick monkey."

"Speaking of which, is Matt up?"

"In the downstairs shower. Now go." Malcolm wobbled down the hall to his parents' master bathroom in his torn leopard print boxers. After a long, soothing shower, and a shave that required two of his father's Gillette disposables, he put on his father's navy blue robe and made his way to the kitchen.

"Better?" he asked.

"Much. Thank you." She flopped three pancakes on a plate and dropped it in his hands. "Sorry, service really isn't my thing."

"So get this. Last night I had a dream we all went swimming down at the KOA. But the pool had sand around the edges, a sort of pool-beach hybrid I guess, and we parked our cars right against the side." Malcolm pointed to Samantha. "You and Monica, plus a writer friend of mine and her husband, you were all wearing these crazy swimsuits from the 1930s or something. Really baggy and saggy. You looked ridiculous."

Samantha rolled her eyes but said nothing.

Matthew hadn't bothered looking up from his *Wall Street Journal* and was finishing off his second helping of scrambled eggs.

"Oh, Matt, that reminds me," Samantha said, dropping the spatula in the sink. "Monica called while you were in the shower."

"Thanks," his eyes were still scanning the stock reports. "I'll call her in a bit." He hoped for long-overdue good news.

"When's she coming?" Malcolm asked.

Samantha tapped him on top of the head with a fork and shook her head at him.

"She's not," Matthew said.

"Not coming?"

"That's what *not* means."

"Sorry there, pal, just asking. I assumed she'd be at our parents' funeral. You only get one, especially in this case, right my man?"

"Just shut up, all right?" Matthew stood and placed his plate and glass in the sink. "Thanks for the eggs, Sam. I've got to run. I need to meet Rain at the church." He walked out the door without looking back.

Malcolm dropped his knife and fork and raised his arms in surrender. "What? Was it the swimsuit thing? In fairness, Monica looked better than you did. Your rear was pretty droopy."

Samantha turned her back to him and dipped her hands into the soapy dishwater.

"Honestly, Sammie, I was just making small talk."

"Things have changed for him recently."

"How so?" Malcolm asked.

Samantha continued washing the dishes.

"Is it the kids thing?" He shook his head. "Jeez, they've known for like five years they couldn't have kids, right? So why are they still trying? They think a kid will solve whatever problems they have?"

"No, Mal, they're trying to *adopt* now, and it's not that easy, unfortunately. They've been so close the last couple years, so close, and something always happens. And yes, having a child will help. It will keep them home more, together more. At least they think so, and that's all that matters." Samantha cleared the syrup, butter, and juice from the table.

"True enough."

"Keep this to yourself, but Matt said Monica's left the gym she's been working for. She's started her own training company.

Some kind of personal training company. No, *life coaching* she calls it. And diet help I think, too. Anyway she's got her own business now and it's put a huge strain on them. They're never home at the same time."

"So she's not coming to her in-laws mega-funeral because she's got a few fat people to watch over?"

"Mal—"

"No," he cut in. "That's wrong. You know it."

Samantha sighed. She stood behind Malcolm and pulled at the ends of his wet, shoulder-length hair. "Time for a cut."

"No way."

"Malcolm Cooper, you can't go to your parent's funeral looking like Sasquatch. You need a cut."

"Two inches."

"Four."

"Three."

"Fine," she agreed. "Three it is."

Malcolm finished his breakfast and changed into one of the three ragged pairs of shorts he'd hauled from Brazil and his well-worn Milton Nascimento T-shirt. He admired his thick, long hair one last time in the bathroom mirror. He met his sister on the screened porch along the back of the house. "Is there a wait?"

"Come on, let's get this done, Mal. A&P will be over soon to get started on the lunch. This place will be crawling with people."

"So what's the weather been like? It feels awfully warm, even for April."

"We had a mild winter and it's been more of the same this spring. Warm and gorgeous." Samantha tossed him a bright yellow Busch Gardens theme park poncho. "Sorry, it's all I could find. . . . Anyway, be grateful."

"For the poncho?"

"The weather. Good weather means the people traveling can get here safely. People are coming from all over, you know." She opened a heavy black case and removed a pair of scissors and her mother's clippers. "Wow."

"What?" Malcolm forced his head through the poncho's small opening, scratching his ears on the plastic edges.

"Mom never cleaned these out real well. They've still got some of Dad's gray hair in them. Not that he had much." She took a coarse brush from the case and wiped it vigorously across the gray plastic clipper guard. Tiny gray hairs blew into the air and turned metallic, flickering in the light. She selected a comb from a pocket on the inside cover of the case. "Look down." Samantha began pulling the comb through the hair on the back of Malcolm's head. "You've got some gray of your own coming in. It's been a stressful two years for you, hasn't it?"

"I wouldn't use that word. The gray probably comes from Mom."

Samantha continued combing his hair into long, straight lines that fell from the crown of his head. Malcolm was much taller than Samantha, almost fifteen inches, and even seated he was a towering figure.

"It was hard, Mal. Dad had these headaches like nothing you could imagine. Mom said he screamed out in the night sometimes, it hurt so much." Samantha cut several inches of hair and brushed it from his shoulders onto the floor. "I knew it was coming though. The doctor at UVA told him six months ago he had three. Every day was a bonus, I guess. And I know this is different for you. You and Dad were always weird, for whatever reason. Everyone knew you were a mamma's boy. Plus you just haven't been around." Samantha took a step back to examine the angle of his neckline.

"I guess for me it's not even real yet. I look out into that backyard and forget I'm not in South America anymore. I'm home. A few days ago I was drifting down the Amazon alone, taking pictures, writing on my legal pads. I missed it here—you mostly, if I'm being honest—but I was content. I was in a place where people didn't gossip about their floozy neighbors or track people's every move. It's like this huge world of its own with different rules, you know? It's, I don't know, it's just cool."

"Cool?" Samantha pulled his bangs up into the air with the comb and lopped off an inch. "That's the best you can come up with, Writer Boy?"

"You need to come to Brazil some day. You need to meet these people. The natives are humble. They're so sincere. They just live. No complications, you know?"

"Someday, maybe. Why not? They have McDonald's down there?"

Malcolm thought of his beautiful Brazilian friend and smiled. "Yeah, Sis." He smiled wider. "They have Mac Donald's."

Samantha began trimming the unruly hair above Malcolm's ears. He watched tufts of hair land on the slick yellow poncho and slide off his lap.

"Mom and Dad are dead," Malcolm said, pausing as if waiting for the words to disappear from an imaginary teleprompter and be replaced with more believable lines. "I'm about to cross paths with my old chum Nathan and his gang of sycophants. And I'm going to jail. For how long? Six months? A year? More?" He wanted to smile again. He didn't. "And I'm about to be in the same room with Rain."

"It's a lot to handle, isn't it? It's like we're trapped in a TV movie."

Malcolm calculated dates and continued as if not hearing her. "You and me and Matt are all here under the same roof for the first time since when, '83?"

"Sounds right. Mom and Dad's anniversary, I think." Samantha glanced toward a small mirror in the black case but continued cutting. "That was a nice weekend."

"Yeah. It was the time you were finally exposed as a cheater at Scrabble."

"I most certainly am not." She flicked Malcolm's right ear with the comb.

"Ouch! You don't remember Dad's speech? I convinced him you had extra letters in your lap and he said how very disappointed he was. He said Coopers didn't cheat. . . . Even Matt laughed at that. He knew I'd been carefully tossing the squares one at a time on your dress under the table. You stood up to get the phone and like fifteen squares hit the floor." Malcolm laughed. "Good times."

"Yeah, for you." Samantha quickly fired up the clippers. "Just for a little cleanup in the back; your neck hair has a bluebird's nest in it." With long, uninterrupted strokes, she buzzed along the back and sides of Malcolm's head. Before he could react, Malcolm looked as if he could have enlisted in the Marines.

CHAPTER 14

As Samantha swept up the remnants of Malcolm's flowing hair, he struggled to remove the plastic poncho, scratching his ears again as he pulled it up and over his head. He removed his T-shirt and shook the loose hair from the fabric. Malcolm ran his fingers through his chest hair and noticed a few more gray strands than last time he'd paid any attention. He turned on the backyard waterspout, bent down, and ran cold water over his head, vigorously tussling what was left of his hair and mumbling about trust and siblings.

"I won't easily forgive you," he said. "It took me two years to grow that."

"I'm sorry I missed it," a familiar voice said from behind him.

Malcolm pulled out of the heavy stream of water and stood. Rain.

"Sam told me you'd grown it out. I wish I'd seen it long." Rain flashed her natural smile, the one that animated her eyes and involved her forehead; the one Malcolm thought Van Gogh dreamt of at night but never used because he couldn't paint a face beautiful enough to match.

There were hundreds of times in the two years since Malcolm had seen Rain that he had imagined this encounter. What would she say? Would she be wearing the necklace he'd given her on prom night? The one he knew made Nathan crazy when she wore it? Would she say anything at all? Malcolm had wondered too what he would say the first time their eyes met after two years. He'd not looked into them since standing at her door and being denied on the night of the fight at Woody's.

He didn't mean to, but out of sheer habit Malcolm examined every inch of her like a piece of art. Rain's hair was as full of life as he'd remembered. Though Malcolm rarely saw her fuss with it, and no matter the time or day, Rain's full, light-brown hair always looked as if every strand had been deliberately placed in its appointed spot. It didn't matter—messy, matted, wet, gathered into a ponytail, pulled into a bun, stuck to her forehead after a jog on a muggy Saturday morning—it always looked exactly as she wanted it to.

"Malcolm?"

He couldn't help but lose himself in Rain's eyes. They were deep vine green, so vivid; the perfect match to her peach cheeks. Malcolm had been trying to run from those eyes, but hadn't realized until now that for the last two years he'd been living in a jungle of the exact same shade.

"Mal?"

He broke his stare and shook his head almost imperceptibly. "It was quite the hairdo." *I'm an idiot,* he thought, but then feared he might have said it aloud.

"Like I said," her smile widened even further, "sorry I missed it."

Malcolm reached down, turned off the water, picked up a towel, and quickly dried his head, swiping at the streams of water on his shoulders and arms. He grabbed his T-shirt from the ground and pulled it back over his head.

"Don't be," he said, finally breathing more naturally. "I looked like a caveman."

Rain let her smile fall. "I'm sorry about your mom and dad."

"Thanks."

"Can I hug you?"

"Would Nathan be okay with that?" *I'm an idiot,* he thought again. But before he could rebound, Rain crossed to him with her arms open wide and tears building in her eyes. Malcolm had never told anyone, but he loved how her tears seemed to catch in her lush eyelashes. After a few seconds they'd fall to her cheeks and race to her chin. The two embraced and the smell of Rain's perfume sent a wave of goose bumps from the back of his freshly shaved neckline down his shoulders and over his arms.

"I'm sorry about your mom and dad." She whispered it this time.

"Thank you," he whispered back and dropped his arms. Rain's arms followed a few seconds later.

"I'm glad you're here." Rain pulled a handkerchief from the front right pocket of her jeans. She dabbed at her eyes and pulled the handkerchief along her chin and cheekbones. "I'm prepared. I learned the hard way. Thursday I kept wiping my eyes and nose on my sleeve. Can't wait to see my dry-cleaning bill." She gave a small half-laugh.

"Wanna come in?" Malcolm nodded his head toward the back porch.

"Not really. People are already arriving for lunch and I'd like a minute."

"A question?" Malcolm was surprised at how easily he had fallen back into their old routine.

"A question." Rain, too, had missed their shorthand.

"Sure," Malcolm answered. "The swing probably needs a workout."

Rain followed Malcolm across the yard to a wooden two-person swing hanging from a sugar maple tree.

"Samantha and I watched your folks in this swing less than a week ago. Sunday night I think. Your dad was having one of his better days and after dinner Laurel talked him into sitting out here. They sat for an hour, maybe a little longer."

"That's nice. Mom and Dad really loved this swing. Brought it all the way up from Charlottesville." Malcolm pushed off on the ground, gently sending the swing into motion.

"Really? I never knew that."

"A gift from Uncle Joe. I think he made it."

"No kidding."

Malcolm nodded.

"I'm sure your mom thought the next time she'd sit on this swing she'd be alone. Bet she never imagined all this."

"Who could have?"

Rain nodded. "I've wanted to thank you."

"For what?" He pushed off the ground again and they both relaxed into the swing.

"For what you did. For that night. For saving me."

He turned to her. "You don't have to thank me for that, Rain. Anyone would have done the same."

"Maybe. But it came with a big price tag. Not many other people would have done that."

"You're right. No one else would have stupidly gone so far."

"You did do a pretty good job on that guy, didn't you?"

Malcolm shrugged. "He had it coming."

"But did you have to beat up my boyfriend?" She smiled and elbowed Malcolm in the ribs.

"Also had it coming."

Rain shook her head. "I don't even want to know. Jealousy is not your greatest attribute."

They swung and listened as the rope scraped and scratched in rhythm against the thick limb hanging above their heads. Two squirrels chased one another down the tree trunk and across the yard. The April air had the unmistakable smell of early summer.

"He loves me, you know."

Malcolm examined the ground beneath the swing.

"I see a Nathan no one else does. He's driven, and I know that bothers some people. And he steps on people's toes, trust me, I know; but he's genuine and committed."

"To what?"

"To me. To a family. To a good life." She looked across the perfectly manicured backyard to a couple talking on the back steps. "He has dreams and a plan. I admire that. I'm excited to be part of those dreams. I suppose, in a way, his dreams have become mine."

"What about your dreams?" Malcolm asked.

"Give me a house full of children who call me *Mommy*, a man who loves me and who writes me a poem or two now and again, and maybe who can make me a swing like this one, and my dreams will find their way to true."

"Nathan writes you poetry?"

"He tries." She smiled. "He tries." Rain turned to look at Malcolm's handsome profile. "Can I ask you a question?" she asked.

"Just one?"

"No, two actually."

"Fire."

"Why'd you leave?"

Once again Malcolm pushed hard against the ground and sent the swing up higher than before. The branch bent slightly under the motion.

"Choices."

"Choices?"

"We all have choices. I made one. I chose freedom and Brazil over spending months or years or however long it would have been in prison. And I chose not to watch you marry him."

"*Years* in prison?" Rain ignored the latter point.

"With my record? You bet." Malcolm leaned back in the swing. "I went too far. I almost killed that man."

"Yes, but you didn't."

"I punched the Commonwealth's Attorney."

"*Twice.*"

Malcolm smiled. "Your fiancé made a compelling case."

"Nathan *promised* me you would have been treated fairly."

Malcolm looked into the tree branches above them. "Has he ever told you that you were worth it?"

"What?"

Malcolm lowered his feet and gradually the swing slowed, stopped. "You said two questions."

Rain hopped to the ground and faced him. "Why didn't you answer my letter?"

The question was no surprise. Malcolm knew the letter well. He'd always suspected it contained a wedding announcement and, in essence, a good-bye letter. He'd hauled it, unopened, in his duffle bag since the day it had arrived.

"I waited for a reply." Rain studied him, then shook her head. "Your mom sent a package after you'd been in Brazil for a while. She sent you a phone; I went with her to Fairfax to buy it. Before she closed the box, I put an envelope inside."

"I didn't get it. I'm not surprised, they open mail down there all the time, packages especially, looking for American candy, stamps, Nikes. Someone must have taken it. It happens."

"They left a phone and took a letter?"

"It happens." Malcolm couldn't tell her the truth: That he'd been afraid to read it. That just the sight of the envelope hurt. He could imagine that the letter said Rain and Nathan had finally tied the knot, and he knew reading it in Rain's curly-cursive would have kept him from sleeping for months.

"Shame." Rain smiled, but not nearly as brightly as before. "I wish you'd gotten it." She straightened her blouse. "I better get inside. Samantha and A&P probably need my help for lunch." She spun around and walked toward the house.

"Rain?" Malcolm called.

"Yes?"

"Why aren't you and Nathan married yet?"

Rain sighed. "Timing." She turned and continued walking.

"Rain?" he called again.

"Yes?"

He stared. "Nothing."

Rain waved and walked away again.

Malcolm sat on the swing. Even outside, even with the smells of the Valley swirling in the wind around him, he could still smell Rain's subtle perfume.

Idiot.

CHAPTER 15

It didn't take long for lunch to become about more than just remembering Jack and Laurel. Over twenty former guests descended on *Domus Jefferson* and the spirit of the Inn resembled a family reunion. Many of the guests already knew each other from having crossed paths over the years, and Rain and Samantha introduced those that didn't. A few had stayed only a few times but had had such a memorable experience they felt an obligation to return and honor the family.

While the crowd ate Virginia ham on homemade rolls and mountainous portions of Rain's potato salad, A&P told vividly detailed stories from her nights at the Inn. Some anecdotes brought laughs, some brought the energetic room to a reverent silence only interrupted by sniffles and the unmistakable crisp sound of Kleenex being pulled from a box.

Samantha proudly introduced her ten-year-old daughter, Angela.

"Hi, everyone," she said.

"She's got the brains of her father and the looks of her mother," Samantha declared.

A&P introduced Joy and Moody Faulkner to the crowd. Joy and Moody had stayed at the Inn for two nights in the spring of 1982 and so enjoyed themselves that Moody resigned as a partner in a high-powered law firm in Washington and the couple bought their own B&B in the majestic Canaan Valley of West Virginia.

"We couldn't believe how generous Jack and Laurel were," Joy explained. "We called to let them know we were making an offer on a place near Timberline Resort. We just wanted some tips on advertising, pricing, that sort of thing, you know? They put Rain in charge, that right, Rain?"

"Yes, ma'am," Rain nodded from her spot in the doorway to the kitchen.

"They put Rain in charge for a couple days here, and Jack and Laurel personally drove all the way out to us. It was right after we closed the deal, wasn't it, dear?" She looked at Moody and patted his knee. He sipped a 7-Up and nodded. "They spent two or three days with us. We couldn't have learned that much in ten years if we'd read every book and magazine ever published about running a B&B. Laurel even suggested the name: *Harmony Woods*. It was perfect, remember, dear?" She patted her husband's knee again. "What people God made in the Coopers. What people. Who goes to such lengths for strangers?"

"Maybe no one," Rain interjected. "But you *weren't* strangers. It only takes one stay at *Domus Jefferson* to become family." Rain raised her glass of water in a toast.

"Here, here," the entire room said as if rehearsed, raising their paper cups high. A&P raised her Maglite instead.

Matthew welcomed the Morgans, a couple from Liberia who'd moved to Reston, Virginia, and were regular Valentine's Day visitors. They, in turn, introduced their children: Tim, Lisa, and Kimberly.

"We might have just raised the minority population of Woodstock by a hundred percent," someone joked.

"Maybe we ought to move here permanently, then," Mr. Morgan teased right back. "A little diversity might shake up this crowd."

Matthew said that this was exactly the kind of magical power the Inn possessed. It could bring people together; it made instant families.

Mrs. Morgan nodded. "It's why we've kept coming. Even seeing Jack and Laurel only once a year was enough to feel like we belonged, like we were family, even though we shared no blood."

"Instant family," A&P said. "You got that right."

Samantha stepped in from the edge of the room and sat next to Kristen Birch on the fireplace. "Where's Layne?" she whispered.

"He couldn't come. Work."

"Everything all right?"

"Everything's great. Layne got a new promotion a few months back and he couldn't get the time off. But we're great, better than ever I think."

"I'm so happy. And how's Kay?"

"She's at Brown, just started last September. She's homesick, I hear it in her voice on the phone *every night,* but she was definitely ready to move on and grow up. And now the nest is empty."

"And do you have that syndrome?"

"Ha! If this is an illness I've never been happier to be sick. We sleep until nine and sometimes lounge in our pj's for days at a time." The women giggled.

"You know what, Kris, would you mind if I told your story?"

"Of course not. I'd be honored."

Samantha stood on the hearth. "Hey folks, do you all know Kristen?" A few heads bobbed up and down, most looked curious. Samantha placed her hand on Kristen's shoulder. "Kristen is a dear friend of ours. She's come up from Roanoke."

"Hi, everyone," Kristen said meekly.

"About, what, ten years ago?"—Kristen nodded and Samantha continued—"she and her husband, Layne, came through Woodstock with their son, Cameron, and their daughter, Kay. Cameron was being treated for cancer, brain cancer of all things, and it didn't look good." Kristen wrapped an arm around Samantha's knee and leaned her head against her leg. "Cameron was a junior in high school and he was a brilliant, brilliant young man. He was a National Merit Scholar."

"Congratulations," said someone from across the living room, recognizing the significance of the honor.

Kristen mouthed a teary-eyed, *thank you.*

"If you looked up *history buff* in the dictionary, you'd see a picture of Cameron, in a shirt and tie no less. He especially loved the Civil War-era. He loved, *loved* Stonewall Jackson and knew everything there was to know about the General."

"So true," Kristen said softly, nodding her head, replaying those days just as she had thousands of times since.

"Every time they drove into D.C. for treatment they would pull off Route 81 and spend the night. Cameron and Dad talked for hours about the history of this area, the history of all these little map-dot towns. He even called Dad *grandpa* a time or two. I think Dad liked that. They had a kinship, I think that's the word. . . .

"After Cameron's last treatment the hospital told Kristen and her husband they had two choices. Their son could be admitted and treated for the pain, but he'd never leave. Or he could go home and pass on privately." Even the four or five small children in the house had stopped to listen. Only Malcolm had disappeared. A&P looked around and wondered if the room had ever held so many people.

"Cameron came up with a third option," Samantha continued. "Without his own folks knowing, he called Dad and asked if he could stay here for a few days. The doctor had said he only had a few weeks, maybe a month, but Cameron knew otherwise, didn't he, Kris?"

"He sure did. And I could have throttled that boy when I found out what he'd done." The anxious room released a collective, quick laugh. Kristen wiped her eyes.

"Some of you know this already, and those that don't won't be surprised to hear that Dad and Mom opened up three of the seven bedrooms for the Birches for as long as they needed them. That first day Dad drove Cameron and Layne up and down Route 11 to see all the historic sites. Cameron wanted to go all the way in to Manassas to see the battlefield at Bull Run, but he just didn't have the strength." Samantha hesitated. "Cameron was weak. Getting weaker by the hour it seemed to everyone. By the third or fourth day, Cameron couldn't get out of bed. His mom and dad   "

Samantha began choking on the words. As she gathered her breath to push on, Malcolm appeared in the doorway and carefully stepped over and around the guests who were sitting on folding chairs or the floor. He handed a folded piece of *Domus Jefferson* stationery to his sister and took a seat next to Kristen.

Samantha read the first paragraph or two and bent down to whisper something in Kristen's ear. After a moment or two Kristen took the note and stood. Samantha took her place on the hearth and slid in close to her brother. Malcolm put his arm around her and lovingly pulled her head onto his shoulder.

"I know there are lots of stories here this afternoon," Kristen took a deep breath and exhaled the words. "I hope you'll indulge me."

February 11, 1979
Laurel,

I know, it's Sunday. Sometimes I guess we make exceptions. If anyone deserves it, it's Cameron.

This has been the most wonderful week. It's been hard, has it ever. But I'm glad we've done this. I'm so glad he asked. No, not glad, honored.

While you were out this afternoon walking with Sammie I called and had Pastor Braithwaite come by to visit with Cameron and his folks. I didn't stay in the room, but the Pastor was crying when he came downstairs. He just looked at me for the longest time, like he couldn't find the words. Then he said that he'd never met a soul more ready to meet God. He said he prays he'll be that ready someday.

You know most people would blame God. I think I would.

I would have told you this earlier if I'd thought I could have without crying. You know me and crying in front of people. After dinner, while you were washing dishes, Layne came down and said Cameron had asked to see me. I walked in and sat on the edge of his bed. His mom and dad left for a moment, but they really didn't have to.

Cameron thanked me for this week and for everything. He also told me to give you a big kiss later. (He smiled really big when he said that, by the way.) Cameron then took my hand, it must have taken every drop of energy that boy had, but he took my hand and placed an 1865 two-cent coin on my palm. He said, "You can have this." It had been his lucky charm ever since being diagnosed a year ago. He bought the coin at a shop in Roanoke the day before they drove up for the first round of tests.

So Cameron placed his palm on top of my hand and said, "Mr. Cooper, sometimes lucky charms just don't work." Then he smiled again. "At least that's my two cents."

I laughed right out loud and kissed that boy on the cheek. We both cried until I worried his body couldn't take it anymore. I composed myself and helped him wipe the tears from his eyes and cheeks. I hugged him one last time and I told him he needed to be with his family. As I pulled the door open I turned to see Cameron had twisted his head and was looking into the lamp on the corner table.

Laurel, I wouldn't have believed it if I hadn't heard it for myself, but as sure as I am writing this, as sure as you're in the next room watching Letterman guest hosting on The Tonight Show, I know what I heard.

Cameron opened his eyes, they were brighter than I'd seen all week, and in a cracked whisper he said, "Stonewall?"

It couldn't have been but ten minutes later that Kris, Layne, and little Kay came downstairs and Layne asked me to make the call. Cameron was gone.

I know death isn't usually a time of joy, but as I write these lines I cannot deny the peace in my heart. I cannot deny that Cameron is free now. I cannot deny that despite the emptiness his family feels, their hearts know the truth. Cameron is where he should be.

I imagine he's already passed through the gate and is walking the foggy fields in Manassas at Bull Run. But he's not walking alone. Stonewall Jackson is there.

Now I know why the Lord took his day off on Sunday. That must be the day he personally greets his favorites.

Jack

Kristen stepped off the hearth and was mobbed by the entire room. One by one they hugged her, even those who moments earlier had never seen nor heard of her. She greeted each gratefully. "Thank you. . . . Thank you so much. . . . This isn't about Cameron, this is for the Coopers. . . . So good to meet you. . . . I just wish Layne were here. . . . You're so kind, thank you." Eventually the guests dispersed to various corners of the Inn for more conversations and catching up. Two couples chatted and took turns on the outside swing.

A&P cleaned up and excused herself. "Castro and I need a walk and maybe a rest before the viewing. And if there's time I need to buy some flashlights." She stopped and turned back at the door. "See you kids in a few hours."

"Love you, Anna Belle," Samantha called. A&P blew her a kiss and shut the door behind her.

"Good woman," Malcolm said.

"The best," his sister answered.

The living room, bursting with mourners just moments before now held only Matthew, Samantha, Malcolm, and Rain. The latter two played checkers on the coffee table.

"Maybe we should talk about the letters," Matthew said.

Samantha spoke first. "I agree. Mal?"

"Sure, I was planning on getting back in there once the place cleared out."

Samantha caught Rain's puzzled look. "Get this, Rain, we found some letters last night. There are probably hundreds of them—"

"Thousands," Malcolm interrupted. "King me." He slid a red checker into a red corner square on Rain's side of the board.

"He's right," Matthew added. "There could be a couple thousand. It looks like Dad wrote our Mom every Wednesday."

"Every Wednesday?" Rain looked incredulous.

Matthew nodded. "It's quite a treasure trove. Not all the letters are horribly exciting, and some are short, just a line or two, but as far as we can tell so far, he wrote Mom every single week."

"That's . . . that's beautiful." Rain felt a lump move from her chest to her throat.

"King me again," Malcolm said.

"Cheater," she whispered.

"I think we should finish reading them and then maybe have them put into a big book," Matthew said. "I've got a friend in publishing that might have some ideas. Maybe we could get them bound in leather with copies for all of us."

"I'd like that a lot, Matt," said Samantha.

"Sounds great," Malcolm said, double-jumping Rain's black checkers and clearing her two remaining pieces from the board. "I'm sure you can send mine in care of the county jail."

Rain threw a checker at him. "I think a book is a wonderful idea, Matthew. I'm sure your parents would want that." She stood from the floor and stretched. "Winner picks up, big man," she told Malcolm. "I'm going to head home, too. Nathan and I are going for a walk before heading over to Guthrie's for the viewing. Want me to take the Bible, Sam? So you don't have to worry? I'll probably beat you there anyway."

"That would be great," Samantha answered, "I think it's on Dad's nightstand."

Rain skipped up the stairs.

"Bible?" Malcolm asked.

"Rain thought it would be nice to have it on the table at the viewing tonight, if that's okay with you two."

"Of course," said Matthew.

Upstairs, Rain lifted Jack's Bible from the nightstand and noticed an envelope sneaking out of the top of the book. She pulled it out and read a sloppy, handwritten note on the front, written vertically, top to bottom.

✉

For Rain Only—My sweet friend, please care for this and give to my attorney, Alex Palmer. You're a rare gem. Will miss you.

> *Jack*
> *(Watch out for Malcolm for me.)*

✉

"Oh my," she gasped. She quickly returned the letter to its place in the Bible and returned downstairs.

"I'm off then," Rain said.

"Thanks again, Rain, we couldn't have done the lunch without you." Samantha and Rain hugged.

Rain blew kisses through the air. "See all of you later."

Samantha poked Malcolm. "Knucklehead. Walk her out."

He saluted and followed Rain to her car.

"Why, thank you, sir," Rain offered as she stepped inside her car and shut the door. She turned the key and rolled down the window. She looked into his eyes and saw Jack.

"I meant to ask earlier, did you finish your book?"

"Book?"

"Oh, come on, your novel, your masterpiece."

"Not quite."

"You making progress, Hemingway?"

"Great, comparisons to a guy that killed himself. Thank you, thank you so much."

"I was comparing the talent, Mr. Cracker Wise."

"Mr. Cracker Wise?"

"Wise Cracker, you knew what I meant." Rain's teeth dazzled.

"Rain, you're sweet, but that's not fair to old Ernest. He was the master."

Rain cocked her head to one side and her hair fell from its familiar spot tucked behind her ear. "Are you ever going to let me read what you've written?"

"Maybe if you visit me in jail."

"Malcolm!"

"Oh, I'm kidding, you don't have to visit."

"You'll never change." Rain stole a glance at her watch, but her smile invited Malcolm to prolong the conversation.

"It's the old classic story: boy meets girl, falls for her as a kid, chases her for years."

"For years?" Rain raised her eyebrows.

"For decades, in fact. He chases her to Brazil where she's doing volunteer work with a church group, building houses, teaching English, and sharing her unmatched skills in the art of Pac-Man."

"Please tell me you made up that last one."

"Buy the book." Malcolm winked.

"May I assume the handsome boy gets the girl?"

Malcolm pointed with both index fingers. "Ha! Who said he was handsome?"

Rain blushed, but only slightly, and no one alive but Malcolm knew her well enough to notice. Rain put on her seatbelt and pretended her mirrors needed adjusting. "Just be sure they both end up happy, no matter what."

"Well, happy endings aren't really my thing, are they?"

"Maybe they should be."

"And maybe I'll finally get one of my own one day." Malcolm shrugged.

Rain reached out through the window and took Malcolm's hand. "Happy endings come in different packages, remember that." Rain rolled up her window and waved good-bye.

Malcolm watched her descend the driveway and turn onto Route 11.

Rain watched him in the rearview mirror.

"Well?" Samantha asked when Malcolm returned to the living room.

"Well, what? Let's read."

They retook their places around the dining room table.

March 30, 1988
Laurel,

It is an unnerving feeling. This could be the last letter I ever write. I feel I've already overextended my expiration date, like bad milk in the fridge after vacation. How's THAT for an analogy? Now you know what to put on my tombstone.

I can't help but wonder, what more do I have to do here? How far behind will you be? Ten years? Twenty? Your mother died at 101. I don't care how wonderful heaven is, I won't be content waiting thirty years for you. Maybe take up smoking to mourn my death. (But not in the house, please.)

Other questions on my mind:

When will I be judged? Only when He comes again? What will I do?

How will I find my parents?

Will you meet someone after I'm gone? Someone more kind? Someone more handsome? Someone more patient? A better kisser?

Where will I wait for you?

Laurel, how long will you be?

Forever,

Your husband

P.S. Is there a VIP area in heaven? Someplace where I can meet the Chicago Cub's Gabby Hartnett? Or better yet, Thomas Jefferson?

P.P.S. Seriously, how long will you be?

July 4, 1956
Laurel,

Maybe it was the fireworks. I'm awake in the middle of the night writing this at the kitchen table. It's been a while since I've had the nightmares this bad.

Tonight I saw Joe die in a foxhole again. He was reading one of my letters and sitting with his gun at his side. A Japanese soldier jumped in and started screaming something, I think in French.

It was real, as always, and I couldn't help Joe because I didn't have a gun. I watched the whole thing from the next foxhole over. The killer wiped his knife on Joe's pant leg, waved to me, and then he just walked away.

I take comfort in knowing the nightmares don't come every night, or even every week anymore. But when they do, I feel like I'm there again. Even though I never was.

I'm sure it was the fireworks.

I think I'll call Joe tomorrow.

Love you,
Jack

February 15, 1956
Laurel,

This is the sort of conversation we should have face-to-face, but it's not that simple. Some things are still easier to talk about on paper.

Last night was enjoyable. The dinner. The music. You do love red roses, don't you?

I must admit I hoped the night would end differently. It's been three months since Malcolm was born and you're still not yourself. I miss you. I miss the intimacy we were getting so good at! (You better be smiling.)

I'm ready when you are. But no rush, having a baby does things to you physically and emotionally that no man could ever understand. But hopefully soon you'll feel well enough for a romantic evening.

Maybe a weekend away? Say the word and I'll put something together and find someone to stay with the boys.

I love you.

Jack

July 16, 1980
Laurel,

Not the most exciting week. I'm not complaining though, last week's letter was a book. Not an interesting book, mind you, but still a book.

Malcolm and Sammie went to dinner last night, just the two of them. When's the last time that happened? I've got my money on Malcolm needing love advice. He never talks to his old man about that sort of thing. I wish he would.

Speaking of money—We betting on the race again this year? Reagan looks strong. That Bush character doesn't have what it takes to be president. Plus, I think he's soft on abortion and the right wing of the party couldn't possibly support that. Reagan's going to turn him into mush before this race is over. And it's hard to picture your man Carter turning it around. He'll be farming peanuts again next summer, mark my word.

If you want I'll let you off the hook for now, but come October I'll need you to ante up. $1, as always.

Love,

Jack

December 18, 1985

LC,

Only a week before Christmas. So much left to do. I love when Christmas falls on Wednesdays, as will be the case this year. That means a long letter next week.

So, because I'm falling asleep at my desk, a short letter tonight. I am exhausted.

I love you dearly.

Jack

P.S. The kids' shelter in D.C. called today to thank us for the check. They're buying a Christmas tree and gifts with it. God bless A&P.

June 16, 1971

Dear Laurel,

Happy anniversary! I always love the years when our anniversary *falls on a Wednesday. It means you get more than a $.99 card from the drugstore. (I know, you can keep saying you love whatever I give, but your face tells me otherwise when Wednesdays roll around!)*

It's been a while since I've worked on this list. Today seems as appropriate an occasion as any to add a few items.

Things I love about you:

1. Your hair. It looks like it did when we married. How is that possible? I think I've been fighting gray since high school.

2. Your laugh. The loud one—not the courtesy giggles—but the belly laugh that fills the Inn and brings guests out from their rooms to see what they're missing. They have no idea.

3. Your sense of fairness.

4. Your patience.

5. The way you let go of the blanket during the night when you roll over so you won't pull it off me. I can tell when you grab it again on the other side and give it a little tug. I like the tugs.

6. Your imagination.

7. Your ability to forgive.

8. Your love of God.

9. The way you drive like you have someplace to go—quickly.

10. The way you look in the late afternoon sunlight when you're tending one of your rosebushes.

11. The way you love our children.

12. Your French toast.

13. The way you listen to me as I ramble on in bed—even when I know you want to go to sleep.

14. Your purr.

15. Your feet.

16. Your politics. We don't always agree, but I love that you care about the system more than most people do.

17. The way you find and keep friends. It's a gift.

18. Your speeches at PTA meetings.

19. Your eyes just before I lean in to kiss you, just before they close.

20. You.

> *I love you.*
> *Jack*

November 1, 1956
Laurel,

This may be the last letter I'll ever write you. I'm not sure why I'm bothering. I suppose because I keep my promises.

I hope you saved the first letter I ever wrote. Find it. Read it.

I just realized it's not Wednesday. Maybe that's appropriate.

Malcolm turned one today.

It rained this afternoon, almost two inches in two hours.

Malcolm took his first steps last night. Is that what prompted you to talk? Guilt at seeing me beam over his accomplishment?

I only write these things so that when you read this letter years from now the day—this day—is crystal clear.

What do you say when you discover your wife has lied to you? What do you say when you feel your life is taken right from your chest, even though I miraculously find myself still breathing?

Am I the last to know?

What am I expected to say? What were you hoping I would say? How have you lived with this? How have you lived with me?

I don't know where I'll be for the next few days. When or if I'm ready, I'll talk.

Please don't look for me. That's the very least you can do.

Jack Cooper

CHAPTER 17

S ilence.

Matthew and Samantha stared at one another. Malcolm held the letter in his hands and fought the urge to curse and scream and flip the dining room table over. Mostly he resisted the need to cry. He carefully set the letter down on the pile nearest him and politely excused himself for the bathroom.

"What . . . was that?" Samantha said slowly.

"I have no idea, not an inkling."

"Matt, you're the oldest, what the heck happened?"

"Please. I was five years old in 1956. I can barely remember the house we lived in."

Samantha leaned back and craned her head, checking on the bathroom door. "Did Mom *cheat?* Is *that* what this is about?" But before waiting for an answer, Samantha began frantically flipping through nearby stacks of letters. "November '56. November '56," she muttered.

"Sam," Matthew said, "maybe we shouldn't—"

"Shouldn't what?" Malcolm asked, reentering the room. His face had been washed. A few stubborn drops of water clung to his forehead.

"Malcolm," Matthew inhaled and placed his hands flat on the table, "let's not get ahead of ourselves here."

"Mom cheated."

"We don't know that. We don't know. Let's calm—"

"Mom cheated, Matt. Read the letter again."

"We don't know, Mal, we—"

"She cheated!"

"Mal—"

"She *cheated* on Dad!" Malcolm shouted. "And he *stayed*!" He exhaled and seemed to shiver. "He stuck around. I don't be—"

"Malcolm—" Samantha stood and placed her hands lightly on his taut arm muscles.

"—I don't believe it."

"Mal, let's keep reading. Obviously there's more here. Obviously whatever happened was smoothed over. All was forgiven." Her eyes found his. "Right? Let's keep reading. We have to."

Matthew watched the scene unfold like the night's last, blurry dream before the sun wakes the house and its dreamers. He dreamt the empty chair next to him held Monica.

Malcolm sat and pushed his stack of letters to the middle of the table, lay his head down, and surrendered to a screaming migraine. He hated his mother.

Samantha pulled another letter from an envelope postmarked LIBERTYVILLE, ILLINOIS, 11/08/1956.

November 7, 1956
Laurel,

I'm in Chicago. I took the train to my mother's. I walked by Wrigley Field yesterday but it was dark and empty. Like me.

Mother and I stayed up last night talking. She's angry I'm here, but glad I came here instead of somewhere else. She thinks I should have stayed with you, fought, demanded answers. She also thinks I should have done more listening. But she's always thought that. Dad was a horrible listener.

There has been a voice in my head (or maybe my gut) that's told me something was missing between us the last year or two. Maybe I haven't been listening closely enough to that voice either.

You sobbed on the day Malcolm was born. Do you remember how much you cried? The nurses were so concerned they wanted to sedate you. I convinced them it would pass.

We all thought you suffered from depression, the kind women get sometimes after childbirth. The crying. The mood swings. You've not been the Laurel I knew since we found out you were pregnant.

At least now I know why. Depression and guilt must look very similar.

Were you aching because of the truth?

Does Ally know? Do your parents know? Do any of our pastors through the years know?

Does anyone else know?

And the question I should have asked before breaking that picture and storming out—

Do you know who Malcolm's father is?

Jack

She cheated," Malcolm said again, calmly. Matthew and Samantha looked at one another across the mountain of letters. Samantha whimpered.

"Malcolm," Matthew said and waited for his brother to face him. "This doesn't change anything."

"Excuse me?"

"It doesn't change anything. It doesn't change you."

"It doesn't change me? It doesn't *change* me?"

"You're a Cooper. Dad loved you. He and Mom survived this."

"But this doesn't change things? Finding out our mother cheated?" Malcolm's voice rose with each question. "Finding out I'm a bastard?"

"I think Matthew means you're *still* our brother," Samantha added. "We still love you. Mom and Dad loved you. You know that."

"All these years," Malcolm stood, "all these years I loved Mom, and all those times I fought with Dad—telling him he was too strict, too demanding, accusing him of always being all wrapped up in honoring the family name—and he knew the whole time I wasn't even his."

"That's right, Mal," said Samantha, sharply. "Dad knew, and yet he loved and raised you. He knew. You said it yourself: *He stayed.*"

Malcolm swiped wildly back and forth across the top of the table sending letters and envelopes flying into all corners of the room. *"He is not my father!"*

He walked toward the front door. "And Mom was a liar," he said as the door shut behind him.

"Where are you going? Malcolm?" Samantha called, her stomach aching.

"Let him go," Matthew said as he knelt to gather his parents' history from the dining room floor. "Let him go."

Five minutes later two tourists on Route 11 picked up Malcolm. They left him at Woody's.

Matthew and Samantha reorganized the letters as best they could and the project soon spread from the top of the dining room table to the china cabinet, the windowsills, and the seats of the other eight dining room chairs. The two said very little. And though she'd not yet read them, Samantha took extra care to safeguard the letters from 1956 and 1957.

"Look, Sammie," Matthew rippled the silence blanketing the room. "Poems." He handed four letters across the table. "Remember these? Christmas, 1958. Mom put copies in our memory books."

December 24, 1958
Sammie and Her Coat of Many Colors
For my daughter, SAMANTHA
on our first Christmas together, 1958

I'd buy you a coat of your own,
but there is no cloth beautiful enough
to knit what you deserve
and no wealth to afford it.

I'd buy you a coat of your own,
but there are not enough colors in this world
to match your spirit
and no rainbow bright enough.

I'll buy you a coat of your own
in heaven.

December 24, 1958
The Fifth Season
For my wife, LAUREL
on our tenth Christmas together, 1958

With each spring comes new life,
energy and green growth.
In summer comes the sun, warm, kind,
and enduring.
Fall brings its canvas of color in careful,
gentle change.
Winter brews into faithful strength,
beauty in pure white.

And then comes you.

You are all that Nature offers,
a blessing, a gift from Father.

You are the fifth season.

December 24, 1958
The Answer
For my son, MATTHEW
on our eighth Christmas together, 1958

"What do you want to be when you grow up?"

From within his sterling smile the order sometimes changes.
But the answer never does.

*"A doctor, a policeman, a Chicago Cub, a TV man,
and a man. Can I?"*

*From Dad's slowly wrinkling smile the wording sometimes changes.
But the answer never does.*

"You can."

December 24, 1958
<u>*The Dream*</u>
For my son, MALCOLM
on our fourth Christmas together, 1958

*Each night in a dream
a wrinkled old man of philosophy
whispers in my ear,
"The perfect ones can be taken home early."*

*Each morning the new dawn
opens my sleepy, worn eyes
and sweeps me down a long hallway toward a small bed.
There's a boy in it.*

He is my son.

*And though I am only tending him,
I pray He will let us keep the boy another day.*

CHAPTER 19

The doorbell startled them both.

"What time is it?" Samantha asked.

"Four-thirty." Matthew checked his Rolex. "Want me to get it?"

"Thank you."

The doorbell rang again. "Coming," Matthew called on his way to the front door. "I'm coming. Don't people know to just walk in a B&B?" He opened the door and smiled. Allyson Husson.

"Any room at the Inn?"

"Aunt Ally. You made it."

"Yes, I did, young man. And you can start the party now."

"Same old Allyson." He looked down at her red leather boots and all the way up to her pink, big-brimmed hat completely covered with pleated taffeta and topped with a bright white bow dotted with rhinestones. Matthew thought it looked like a hood ornament and considered saying so, but knew Malcolm would make the same joke later. Matthew admired Allyson's silver hair sneaking out from underneath the sides of the hat. Laurel's younger, sixty-one-year-old sister also wore white jeans, a Caesar's Palace denim shirt, and carried an imitation fur coat under her right arm.

Allyson Husson was raised with her sister in Hampton Roads, Virginia, just a few miles from the coast. Their parents would never admit it, but everyone knew Allyson was the result of a wonderful accident. Their parents divorced while the girls were still in school: Laurel was in the eleventh grade, Allyson the second. After the divorce, though, their mother slipped into a depression heavier than Hampton Roads' humid sea air. She encouraged her girls to mind their diets, stay thin, wear makeup, learn to cook better than she did, and learn their place in the world. In the years after the split, Allyson decided her place in the world was anywhere other than Virginia. She begged and plotted relentlessly for permission to live with her father, but neither Laurel nor her mother ever let her stay for more than a day or two at his apartment forty-five miles away in Williamsburg. Laurel would only visit her father in her sister's company and refused to spend the night. "My home will always be wherever my mother is," she told her father.

And despite her desires to leave Hampton Roads and pursue education elsewhere, when Laurel graduated from high school she chose to live at home and support Allyson and her mother. She worked at a PX inside the gates at the naval base located within walking distance of their home in a safe, white middle-class neighborhood.

When Laurel wasn't working she was discovering the Bible and sharing the stories with her mother. Laurel read to her, often for hours at a time, and together they found the faith that hadn't been allowed in their home before the divorce.

Allyson's was a different mission. Before bed each night she entertained her mother with silly dance routines and monologues. Laurel once told Allyson that every joke she told added another week to their mother's life. Their mother died with a smile on her face at age 101, some twenty-two years after her alcoholic ex-husband.

Allyson honed her skills as an entertainer on the sidewalks near their home. It was months before either her sister or mother knew that Allyson had been spending afternoons loitering outside the navel base telling jokes to soldiers as they came and went. By the time she was fifteen, Allyson was performing at local clubs on weekends and being billed as the youngest working comedian on the east coast. It probably wasn't true, but Allyson wasn't likely to correct anyone. After dropping out of high school in 1944, a decision that haunted Allyson and broke her sister's heart, Allyson traveled to the West Coast to dig for her break.

Before she knew it, Allyson was in Europe, singing to soldiers on a USO tour. She was on stage in London on May 7, 1945, singing Doris Day's "My Dreams Are Getting Better All the Time," when an American journalist stormed into the club, leapt to the stage, and announced that the Germans had surrendered. Then he kissed Allyson on the mouth. They were married in Los Angeles six weeks later.

Allyson was single again by 1949. She married a B-movie actor in 1952; was divorced in 1954; married a lounge singer in 1958; divorced again in 1963; and married for the final time in 1969 to her true love, a casino-building contractor. That storybook marriage ended in 1979 in Las Vegas when a wayward wrecking ball crushed her husband's onsite work trailer.

That was the same year it was her turn to find God.

There was no choice for Matthew but to smile. "Wow, you . . . you look really good." He noticed her fur coat.

"Don't worry," Allyson said. "It's not real. It's from fake minks."

"In that case, come on in." Matthew reached for her suitcase.

"Put that down," she ordered. He obeyed. "Hug your aunt." He obeyed again. "You're Jack Cooper's son, no doubt about that. He was never one to hug me either."

"I'm sorry," he said, but his mind was still on Malcolm.

"Now let me go, you're married . . . and grab that suitcase."

By the time he picked up Allyson's bag for the second time and turned to enter the house, Allyson was halfway down the hallway.

"Samantha, Malcolm, I'm here."

"Dining room," Samantha beckoned.

"There's my little actress," Allyson said, entering the room. "Hug me."

Samantha stood and also obeyed.

"I am so hurt for you kids."

"Oh Aunt Ally, we're fine. We're all fine."

"Um," she hesitated and raised her thin eyebrows, "no you're not. No one loses their mother and father in one fell swoop and is *fine* about it. You're not fine. But I'm here to help." Though hardly possible, she hugged Samantha even harder.

"You're the best. And I'm sorry for you too. You've lost quite the sister."

"Yes, I have. But I'll find her again. It's been five years since I've been out here, and at my age I'm likely to see her sooner now than if we were both still kicking around on opposite sides of this rock."

Samantha smiled but the tears returned. "I've really missed you." She released one hand and moved it up to wipe her nose.

"Use the shirt. That's why I wore it. You ever eaten the Caesar's buffet?"

Samantha laughed and cleared a pile of letters from the nearest chair. Allyson sat and removed her gargantuan hat, hanging it on the chair next to her. "So where are we?"

"Where are we?" Samantha asked.

"Schedule, darling. What's the latest?"

"Ah. We're heading to the viewing soon, need to be in Edinburg by 6:00, takes just a few minutes. Tomorrow there's a concert at the church in the morning, then a brunch you're welcome at, of course, and the funeral is tomorrow evening back at the church."

"I put your bag upstairs in the master bedroom, that okay?" Matthew reentered the dining room and retook his seat at the table. Allyson looked puzzled. "You *weren't* planning on staying here?"

"No. Well yes," she corrected, "yes, of course. I just thought you would put me in another room."

"It's the nicest room in the Inn, Ally. Mom and Dad would want you there."

She lowered her voice. "Then thanks, Matt. Thanks very much." She brushed a tear away from her cheek and then picked up a letter from one of the stacks on the table. "What's all this?"

Matthew looked at Samantha. She nodded. "Did you know that Dad wrote love letters?" He gestured across the table with both hands.

"Oh, you mean the Wednesday Letters."

"You knew?"

"I was your mother's best friend as well as her sister; of course I knew. She called me from her honeymoon and read me the very first one. I wished my first husband had been like that. Someone who poured his heart out without being asked? Pretty rare." She studied Laurel's name on a pale green envelope. "Well, it took me a few tries, but I found that man eventually, and I'll carry his last name with me to my own grave." She admired her fourth wedding ring and first real diamond she'd ever worn.

"Your mother didn't share many letters with me, they were personal you know, but from time to time she'd call and read something clever to me. She loved these letters, and she was proud of your dad for writing them. I imagine there are pyramids full of treasure in these letters, some whispered secrets, adventurous accounts you kids never knew about, even some juicy gossip."

Allyson reached for the closest envelope and removed a letter written on Trans-World Airlines stationery. "'July 23, 1969,'" she read aloud. "'Hi Laurel, can you believe a man walked on the moon this week? What a miracle! Will our children see a man live there one day? I think they will. If we can put Neil Armstrong on the moon, what else can we do?'" Allyson quietly and quickly skimmed the rest of the letter and slid it back in its envelope.

"Those two lived quite a life," she mused. "These pieces of paper," she tapped the top of a letter with her index finger as she spoke, "they saved their marriage more than once."

Allyson looked at Samantha then peered across the table at Matthew. His olive eyes were fixed on hers. She looked back to Samantha.

"I wonder if letters like this would have saved my first marriage. Kids, have I ever told you about my first husband, Darwin?" She didn't wait for an answer. "He was a good man, but for whatever reason he stopped loving me. I'm not sure why. I always figured I wasn't smart enough for him. But I tell you what, I do not, *do not* regret those years. I learned so much from him. He was a writer you know, worked for the *New York Times,* even won some awards for his writing. We met overseas as World War II ended. It was from Darwin that I learned about the war, why we really fought. I learned about literature and places in the world I never knew existed. Before Darwin, I wouldn't have known the difference between William Shakespeare and Charles Schulz. I went to high school of course, your mom saw to that, but I wasn't really there." She lost her gaze in the blend of white and aged-yellowed letters and envelopes.

"I met Charles Schulz once, did I ever tell you? Your mom did, too. Charles fought in the war, though I guess at that time just about everyone fought in the war. Except your dad. I guess he fought a different war. Anyway, Darwin and me were living in New York. It was 1948, maybe '49, not long before my divorce. It wasn't much after your mom and dad got married. Your mom hated that, you know, the awkwardness of being a newlywed while I was getting divorced.

"Anyway, Darwin did a story for the *Times* about up-and-coming cartoonists and he heard about this guy in Minnesota working for the paper in St. Paul, I think it was, who was drawing a strip called *Li'l Folks.* This fellow's comic had a dog and a boy named Charlie Brown. Sound familiar? And did you know," she turned to Matthew, "that man, Schulz, saved every cartoon from every June sixth? He treated those strips really special. Saved them in honor of his comrades."

"Normandy," Matthew said.

"That's right, Matthew," she nodded. "Normandy. You know your dad regretted not being there that day. Always did."

"At Normandy?" Samantha asked.

"He was assigned to the shipyard in Portsmouth. Norfolk Navy Yard they call it now, I think. He was so good with his hands. He had the mind of an engineer, he could see things, see how they worked. He could see things no one else could. But your father felt such guilt after the war ended. Really haunted him. Even scared your mom sometimes.

"See Jack knew a lot of boys that died in the war, that died on the beach that day." Allyson briefly lost her gaze in the piles of letters. "I know your Uncle Joe saw some fighting, some action they used to say, but he wasn't there long. He was drunk when he landed back home and has been drinking ever since." She suddenly shifted her gaze to Matthew.

"Jack always thought people looked at him differently for not fighting. He never understood that his work on those ships was every bit as important as carrying a gun in combat. He worked on some of the very ships that carried those boys up to that beach. I remember your mom calling me up after they'd been married a couple months. That was what, '48? Your dad was having nightmares even though he'd never stepped foot off U.S. soil, never seen a man killed during his time in the service. All he'd seen were the newsreels. He'd watch them over and over, even after the war was long finished. He had a few friends who made it home still breathing, but they were different. They went with faces of nineteen-year-old boys and came back looking like forty-year-old men. And Jack didn't know what to say around them. He kept in touch with a couple, though. One I remember because he'd lost an arm. Your mom and dad had him over for Thanksgiving one year. I think, Matthew, you were just a baby then.

"Some people—some of your dad's cousins in Chicago for sure—thought your dad was just . . . lucky. He played baseball in high school. You knew that I bet—he was always playing baseball. The baseball team his senior year won the state championship. That was probably '36 or '37, maybe even '38. I recall your mother saying Jack was a catcher and could hit left- or right-handed, it made no difference.

"Did you know Jack kept a photo of that team? I bet it's up in his room somewhere right now. Your mom said on the back of the photo your dad wrote down the names of everyone on that team and when they died, as best he knew.

"Yes, people said Jack Cooper was lucky, said he was the golden boy, said he was lucky that he never had to strap on a parachute or run up the beach, never had to step over his dead buddies like they had to. Whenever they got together and talked about the war, any war—Korea, Vietnam, it didn't matter—they looked at each other like it was a special club your dad didn't belong to because he hadn't fought.

"Your dad never went to war, not because he didn't want to, but because he'd been blessed with those hands and those eyes that saw things others couldn't. But he suffered all his life from the war anyway. He went through some things." Allyson's voice trembled. "He really did." She rubbed at her eyes.

Samantha and Matthew stood and moved to Allyson's side. They knelt on the floor to her left and right and each wrapped an arm around her shoulders. Allyson placed her hands on Matthew's cheeks and kissed his forehead. He put both arms around her for one last hug, then released her and vanished upstairs.

Samantha and Allyson held each other until Matthew returned with an 8x10 black-and-white photo of eighteen young ball-players in white jerseys with oversized "C's" on their chests and matching caps. They huddled around a large silver trophy of a twelve-inch ballplayer casually cocking a bat over his shoulder. Matthew and Samantha spotted and admired their father, sitting proudly in the center of the bottom row and pointing with both hands at the camera.

Matthew flipped the photo over. There were eighteen names. Next to nine of them the date June 6, 1944, was neatly written in black ballpoint pen. Three others died before the end of 1945. Two died in the late sixties and two more in the mid-seventies.

Only Jack and his twin brother, Joe, an all-star pitcher on that championship squad, had no date scrawled by their names.

Matthew pulled a pen from his shirt pocket and wiped his hand across the back of the photo. Then, next to his father's name, he wrote in small, careful print: *April 13, 1988.*

CHAPTER 20

Saturday Evening

Samantha, Matthew, and Allyson might have sat in the Inn's dining room all night had the phone not startled them. It was Rain.

"Sam, is everything okay? It's almost six, people are worried."

"Everything's fine," said Samantha. "Just lost track of time. Aunt Ally made it in."

"That's great, Sam. So can I tell people you're on your way?"

"Yep. We're walking out the door. See you soon." Samantha and Allyson changed into dresses. Samantha chose a gray wool skirt with a black knit top and Allyson bypassed the wrinkled clothes in her own suitcase to wear one of her sister's modest dresses from the upstairs closet. Matthew put on his favorite suit, a jet-black Armani that Monica had given him for Christmas a few years earlier.

"I'll drive," Samantha said as they descended the front porch stairs and she pointed to her police cruiser. Just as all three doors shut, Matthew and Samantha yelped in unison, "Malcolm!"

"Where is he?" Allyson asked.

Samantha frowned. "Good question."

"Woody's?" Matthew suggested from the backseat.

"Good answer." Samantha peeled out and turned onto Route 11, heading for downtown Woodstock—exactly the opposite direction from the viewing at Guthrie's in neighboring Edinburg.

She hit her lights and siren.

"Anybody seen my brother?" Samantha raised her voice above the Saturday evening noise. "Malcolm Cooper?"

Laurie Loveless, one of the two bartenders on shift, cut her way through the crowd toward Samantha. "Hello, Sam." Her forceful voice belied her petite, charming face and subtle smile.

"Hey, Double L. You seen Mal?"

"He was here an hour ago, didn't stay long."

"Was he drunk?"

"No, and the truth? I'm not sure he drank anythin' at all. Alice served him a soda or somethin'. Said he needed his mind clear. But he was actin' pretty weird, Sam, ramblin' on about being lost, mumblin' about your mom. But like I said, he wasn't here long, half hour maybe."

"Thanks anyway." Samantha patted Laurie's arm and turned to leave.

"Wait," Laurie said. "He asked me if I knew."

"You knew?" Samantha spun around to face her.

"Of course I did, darlin', everyone does by now. It's all over town. Shoot, it's all over the Valley by now." Laurie's voice softened so much that Samantha had to rely on the shape of her thin, red lips for the words. "We're all real sorry 'bout your parents. They were real good people."

Samantha exhaled and replied with a graceful, grateful smile and walked out of Woody's.

"Well?" Matthew asked as Samantha buckled herself back into the driver's seat of her cruiser.

"He *was* here. Now he's not. And I'm more than a little irritated."

Allyson slapped the black vinyl dashboard playfully. "Now this is my kind of adven—"

"Officer Cooper, what's your twenty?" the radio interrupted.

"Woody's on Main. What's up, Barry?"

"I've got something you might want to see."

"Does it have anything to do with my fugitive brother?"

"Yep. And the Woodstock Tower."

Samantha groaned. "We're dopes," she looked over her shoulder at Matthew. "We should have gone there first." She hit the talk button again. "Crescimanno around?"

"No. And I'm not calling him, but word travels."

"On my way." Again Samantha lit up her flashing strobes and flipped on the siren.

"I spoke too soon." Allyson slapped the dash again. "*This* is my kind of adventure."

Samantha sped south down Main Street and then up the winding Woodstock Tower Road.

"Sis, don't you think this is a bit fast for gravel—"

"Matthew, shut it."

"Okay then."

Samantha pulled in behind the other police cruiser and led Matthew and Allyson up the narrow path toward the tower. Officers Keith and Barry stood whispering in the thin foliage to the side of the tower's base.

"Sorry boys," Samantha said. "How'd you find him?"

"Some tourist called 911. Said they'd been up here and a man was singing to himself, acting strangely. They were concerned."

"Malcolm," Samantha called up to him. "You done here?"

"Almost," he shouted down.

"What exactly are you doing?" she asked.

"Thinking."

"About what?"

"Not really sure."

Allyson stepped toward the tower and put her hand on Samantha's arm. "Let me try. Hi, Mal," she yelled louder than she needed to.

"Allyson?" Malcolm answered, leaning over the side and looking down. "That you?" Malcolm's hands felt clammy against the metal railing.

"The one and only. Come on down, would ya?"

Malcolm looked away from her. "Did you know?" he asked, his gaze fixed far across the horizon.

"Did I know what?" Allyson asked.

Malcolm yelled this time. *"Did you know? Did you know your sister was a cheater?"*

"Malcolm! Come down here. Come see me."

"You'll tell me? You'll tell me who I am?"

"We'll talk."

Malcolm paused briefly before beginning to descend the three flights of gray metal stairs.

"Is he drunk?" Allyson whispered to Samantha.

"No. Just broken."

"Well, remember to be kind, Sammie. And you too," she looked to Matthew standing behind them. "Put yourself in his shoes for a bit today." Brother and sister half-nodded to her and then to one another.

Malcolm stepped off the bottom step and walked past the officers. "Fred. Barney," he said politely, nodding at each man.

Allyson met Malcolm and swallowed him in her arms. "I missed you."

Before Malcolm could answer, his chest was shaking and his

hands were gripping the back of the dress Allyson had borrowed from her sister. He recognized both the dress and its smell. He wept.

"It's all right, son. Shhh. It's all right."

Malcolm lifted his face from her shoulder and almost saw the face of his mother. "Did you know?"

Allyson caught the eyes of Samantha and Matthew at the edge of the cruiser. "Yes," she kissed him on the forehead. "I knew."

CHAPTER 21

Samantha parked in a front-row spot at Guthrie's Funeral Home marked by a square, black-and-white metal sign that read *For Deceased Family Only.* She raised a single finger and connected with Malcolm in the rearview mirror. "Don't, Malcolm. No jokes."

All four exited the cruiser.

"I can't believe you're making me show up in shorts and a T-shirt."

"Sorry, Malcolm," Samantha said. "We're already a half-hour late from having to hunt you all around town." She pulled gently on the end of his T-shirt. "Don't worry, brother," she whispered. "People will understand."

Ariek Guthrie, who'd been outside standing guard, saw them standing on the curb and briefly poked his head into a door, presumably to announce their arrival, then waved the group toward the cobblestone path that led to a private entrance near the front of the chapel. "In this door, please, Coopers. We're so glad you made it."

Allyson walked with her arm awkwardly around Malcolm's waist. She tugged at him to walk slower. "Go ahead, you two. We're right behind you."

Samantha took Matthew's hand and stepped through the door Ariek Guthrie held open in the same distinguished way he had hundreds of times before. Ariek slipped in behind them and pulled the door shut when he noticed Malcolm and Allyson had stopped at the head of the path.

"Malcolm," Allyson said, pulling down slightly on his earlobes. "This isn't going to be easy for anyone, least of all for you. I know that. Your brother and kid sister know that, too. But, Malcolm," she tilted his chin up with her fingers so that their eyes met, "this viewing tonight isn't optional. We've got to do this, we've got to stick together, and we've got to keep you straight tonight." She noticed tears again crowding each other in the inner corners of his eyes. "I promise, we'll talk back at the Inn later, all right? We'll talk."

Malcolm dropped his gaze and spoke to his feet. "I don't even know who I am."

Despite her best efforts, Allyson couldn't avoid thinking this once proud, courageous thirty-two-year-old man had been reduced to a confused twelve-year-old boy.

"What's that, honey?"

"I don't know who I am." He shook his head. "How does that happen?" he asked, wiping his runny nose on the tail of his T-shirt. "How does someone find out between lunch and dinner one day that they aren't who they thought they were?"

Allyson considered her response.

"My father is alive." Malcolm clenched his fists deep inside his shorts pockets. "He's alive somewhere. He's not in there."

"Yes, sir, he is," she answered emphatically. "Your father is lying right inside there. He's lying beside your mother." She hugged him again. "Nothing has changed, sweetheart. Jack Cooper is still your father, my sister is still your mother, and they both loved you in ways your mind won't let you see."

"So tell me. Why? Why did he stay? All those letters . . . he just kept writing them, like nothing happened."

"Not so. Something *did* happen, and make no mistake, young man, your father suffered. And so did your mother. Maybe more so."

"Those aren't answers!" His voice rose and cracked.

"Later."

"Tonight?"

"Tonight."

She embraced him a final time. "All right now, let's go inside. And tuck your T-shirt into those shorts, would you dear? This is a viewing, not the Brazilian Carnival."

Despite the migraine and twisting stomach, Malcolm found the energy to smile.

One after another, the visitors paid their respects. They came from the south, from Harrisonburg, Staunton, and all the small towns that guard both sides of historic Route 11: New Market, Mount Jackson, Edinburg, Woodstock, Tom's Brook, and Strasburg. Several traveled from the east in a carpool from D.C., Arlington, and Rosslyn, all nearly a hundred miles away, well inside the famed Washington Capital Beltway.

Mourners paused at the matching pine caskets lined with hand-stitched, creamy white silk. Jack wore a white suit and at last had a pain-free look of contentment on his face. Laurel wore a white dress and light, barely perceptible makeup. Both had their left hand crossed atop their right and resting on their lower stomach. Their wedding rings shone in the soft light.

The caskets were placed on either side of the pulpit in the nondescript, brown-paneled chapel the Guthries had added onto their funeral home in the late 70s.

Pastor Doug stood like an honor guard in a corner with his hands reverently at his side. He occasionally spotted and embraced a particularly friendly or emotional guest.

To the right of the pulpit—and the right of Jack's casket—

stood Matthew, Allyson, Samantha, her daughter Angela, Malcolm and, at Samantha's insistence, Rain.

Pastor Braithwaite from the church in Mount Jackson also attended. He stood at the front door near the Guthries, smiling at faces both familiar and strange and thanking everyone for coming.

Nathan watched closely most of the night from a conspicuous spot just behind the receiving line.

During a brief lull in the line of visitors, Rain leaned over and placed her hand on Malcolm's lower back. "Shorts?"

"Don't ask."

"I won't," she smiled, knowing she'd hear the whole story from Samantha later anyway.

"Thanks."

"I'm really glad you're here." This time she whispered so close to his ear he felt her breath on the back of his neck. Her breath left a trail of hairs-on-end on his skin.

Malcolm ached to take her by the hand and lead her into the parking lot and into the new reality that he was not the son of Jack Cooper. Instead he simply said, "Thanks."

"Don't thank me, just keep being so well-behaved."

"Numbness will do that to a man."

Another dozen visitors stopped to shake hands, including Maria Lewia, Woodstock's museum director. She hugged Malcolm and asked him about his book. She also made him promise he'd visit her office before leaving town again.

At the other end of the line Matthew had perfected his answer for why Monica hadn't made the trip. "She's in Newark. She wanted so badly to be here, but this might be our best chance to adopt a baby. Mom and Dad would have wanted it this way." He wondered if any of it was true, but saying so made the guests' eyes relax. "I'll give her your condolences."

Malcolm studied each face for a sign, some recognition, a clue that they knew more than he did. Malcolm decided either the community knew even less than he did about his history, or that they all belonged at the World Series of Poker. No one gave the slightest hint—not a subtle nudge of understanding, not a knowing arm-squeeze—to suggest they recognized why his pain was different from anyone else's in the room. Even still, he held every hand and every gaze a few seconds longer than was typically comfortable. He looked into people's eyes he'd never bothered noticing before.

He hoped someone knew the truth.

He wondered who might talk.

He wondered who'd been lying to him every time they passed him on the street and said, "Hello."

He wondered if his real father would pass through the line and slip him a note with his hotel phone number scribbled in pencil.

As the minutes crawled by, Malcolm found it comical that he was making such great efforts to portray his grief as something more than the death of his parents. Even Rain, perhaps the person who'd always known him best, stood at his side unaware of the battle between deception, grief, and truth that waged in Malcolm's gut. Once or twice, when Rain noticed Malcolm struggling to balance his emotions, she covertly reached her soft fingers across and squeezed Malcolm's hand long enough to send a bolt of adrenaline through his veins.

Every hour or so Malcolm checked the round wooden clock on the far wall to find than only ten minutes had passed since he'd last looked. "How long do we have to stay?" he asked Samantha during another lull in the receiving line.

"As long as it takes, Mal, until everyone has had a chance to say hello and pay their respects."

Malcolm raised his eyebrows, begging for a better answer.

"Maybe another hour."

"Better." He turned to whisper something to Rain, then looked back at his sister. "I'll be right back."

"Mal?"

"Relax, just hitting the bathroom. You used to call me Mr. Peanut Bladder, remember?"

On his way toward the lobby Malcolm passed Nathan chatting with Gail Andrus, the Shenandoah County Treasurer. Without breaking stride Malcolm said every bit as loud as he meant to, "Rain's all yours again."

Gail thought it was funny.

Nathan did not.

Malcolm stood at one of the two urinals staring up at the ceiling when Pastor Doug quietly walked in and stepped next to him to use the other.

"Oh, hey there."

"Hello, Malcolm."

"It's like a pastors' convention around here."

He smiled. "You have Jack's sense of humor."

Malcolm looked at the wall. "So you come here often?"

"More than I'd like," Pastor Doug nodded and smiled. "I figure I'm getting old."

"You and me both." Malcolm spun around to wash his hands.

"How are you holding up?" Pastor Doug asked, pulling on the soap dispenser lever and working the soap into enough lather to wash every hand in the funeral home.

"I'm still here. That probably counts for something."

"I'd sure say so."

"You knew my parents pretty well, didn't you?" Malcolm rubbed his hands under the hot air dryer.

"I knew your dad mostly. Why?"

"I guess I'm just curious. A lot of the people here tonight are from out of town, older friends like you that probably hadn't seen them in a while."

"And?"

"I don't know. I guess I wonder how many really *knew* them, really knew my mother especially, or if they're just here because they think they're supposed to be."

"Do you think that's why *I'm* here?"

"Not you, I mean the others."

"You might be surprised." Pastor Doug took his turn drying his hands. "Jack and Laurel were well-respected and well-liked in a lot of circles."

"Maybe. But that's different than really *knowing* someone, right?"

"You know better than most that your family has always been private."

Malcolm fished. "How much do you know about their past?"

"Well, I figure your parents weren't perfect—none of us are, after all"—Pastor Doug smiled—"but they sure tried. They were good people. They were kind and forgiving. Together your father and Pastor Braithwaite, my spiritual mentor, got me my first job preaching in Winchester. I would never have known the beauty of this Valley or her people without your father's efforts."

Malcolm nodded.

"Truthfully, I've not seen your father in a bit, but I can tell you he was responsible for a lot of good in this county. Your mother too."

"Right. She was definitely responsible for—"

The door flung open and Nathan Crescimanno entered.

"Malcolm. Pastor." He nodded as he said their names deliberately.

"Pastor Doug, have you met the Commonwealth's Attorney and future governor of the state of Virginia?"

"*Commonwealth* of Virginia," Nathan corrected.

Malcolm smiled.

"We met outside, yes," Doug answered. "Good to see you again, Mr. Crescimanno."

The three men stood in the doorway.

"Well, this is awkward," Malcolm said.

"Is it now," Nathan mumbled, walking into a stall and shutting the door behind him.

Pastor Doug and Malcolm walked back into the lobby together. The two stopped at a table holding four photos of the couple and assorted memorabilia, including Jack's Bible.

After a few moments of surveying the display, Pastor Doug offered, "I figure you two have some history." He picked up a photo of Jack and Laurel on the steps of the Monticello and pretended to look for the third time. "But as someone from the outside, can I ask why you make it harder than it needs to be?"

"How so?"

"Getting under his skin like that. I figure you like to tweak him."

"Nathan's an easy target."

"Maybe he is," Pastor Doug conceded, "but he holds the keys right now, doesn't he?"

Malcolm was perplexed at his interest. It showed.

"I didn't mean to overstep my bounds, I apologize."

"It's okay," Malcolm said. "You mean well."

"Sure do." Pastor Doug hesitated. "You know, Malcolm, no one is perfect."

"Don't I know it."

Pastor Doug put a hand on Malcolm's shoulder. "I think well of your family—of you. We'd like to have you around. I figure your siblings could use you right now."

Malcolm knew it was true.

"When you're ready, come find me."

Malcolm playfully punched the Pastor's shoulder. "I will."

CHAPTER 22

The crowd finally thinned by 10 P.M., and by 10:20 only a few people remained. A&P and Aunt Allyson visited with Mr. and Mrs. Guthrie in the funeral home's adjacent business office and quizzed them over the final logistics for getting Jack and Laurel's bodies to the church for the funeral the following evening.

Angela kissed her mother and uncles good-bye and left to spend the night at the Godfrey's.

Rain and Nathan sat close in a loveseat in a corner of the same room where the Coopers said good-bye to the final hangers-on.

Matthew carefully closed and locked each casket. Then he took his monogrammed handkerchief and painstakingly polished away the shiny canvas of fingerprints on the silver handles and rails until he saw his reflection.

Malcolm and Samantha stood arm-in-arm behind the pulpit and below the painting of Jesus Christ that hung high on the front wall overlooking the caskets. Samantha rested her head on Malcolm's shoulder.

A sliver of Pastor Doug was visible through the open door in the back. He stood in the lobby at the table of family memorabilia and thoughtfully thumbed through the New Testament in Jack's prized Bible.

"Ready to head out?" Matthew asked, jutting his head between Samantha and Malcolm's.

"About two hours ago," Malcolm answered.

"Me too," Samantha admitted. "Let's get out of here."

The three quickly said good-bye and thank you to Rain, Nathan, and both Pastors Doug and Braithwaite.

"Good luck," Rain offered, hugging each of the Coopers as they stood at the door.

"Good luck?" Nathan asked after the door swung shut and the Coopers disappeared down the cobblestone path back to Samantha's police cruiser.

"It's going to be a challenging evening for them as they come to grips with everything, that's all. They've really needed some time alone, just the three of them. I'm glad they will finally get it tonight."

Nathan watched them through the window.

"You okay?" Rain asked.

"Yeah." Nathan shuffled his feet. "It's just difficult. I feel selfish for wanting this weekend to end so we can get back to us. Is that crazy?"

"No, Nate, it's not. You're in a tough spot, I know. But you're doing great."

"You think?"

"I do."

"I can't wait to hear that in another context, you know." He kissed her.

"Patience, Mr. Crescimanno, let's just get through the weekend." Rain stretched her arms around him.

Nathan did the same, hugging her back and then slowly letting his hands slide down around her thin waist to her hips. "You know I love you, right?"

"I know you do."

"I just want a life with you. I want for us to move on and have kids and build a family together, security together, a life together, success together."

"I know, Nate. I want all that, too."

"You sure?"

"I'm sure."

"I've got nothing to worry about?"

"You've got nothing to worry about."

"You *sure* everything is all right?"

"Right as Rain." But outside the window, in the orange glow of a bright streetlight bouncing off the parking lot, she saw the

Cooper siblings standing in a tight circle and discussing matters of life and death. She wished she were among them, at least for the night.

Eventually Samantha and Matthew agreed with Malcolm that, in fact, it was worth driving north from Edinburg to the tiny town of Tom's Brook for milkshakes at the truck stop off Route 81. They reasoned their first choice, Walton and Smoot's Drug Store on Main Street back in Woodstock, was closed by that hour.

"Hey guys," Matthew said from the backseat. "Want to read some letters?" He held a small pile up and waved the papers between Samantha and Malcolm in the front seats.

"Hey!" Samantha's voice rang through the car. "I thought the letters were staying at the Inn."

Matthew shrugged. "I thought we might as well use the time."

"Then why do you sound so guilty?"

Matthew shrugged again.

"You're a bad brother," Samantha added.

"So no?" Matthew asked.

"So yes," Malcolm answered for them all.

February 22, 1961
Dearest Laurel,

I'm sure you're sick of me saying this, but last weekend was a much needed break. To think we've both lived in Virginia our entire lives and never visited Natural Bridge. Shameful. Let's go again. Next week. Think Amanda would watch the kids again so soon? (I'm only half-kidding.)

Speaking of "Natural" Bridge—and I'm writing this with complete knowledge it may someday be read by our children—taking my swimsuit at the hot springs and locking yourself in the car up the hill was an act of war. Did you see the look on that ranger's face? I could have been ticketed! Take note. This is a battle I shall not lose. I will be waiting. You will not know the time or place, but rest assured, Laurel Cooper, before we leave this earth, you too will find yourself mooning the wildlife.

Jack the stRipper

March 1, 1961
Mrs. Cooper,

I always feel a little funny writing my letters when you're sitting across the room. Right now you're reading the book Matthew gave you for your birthday. What sort of ten-year-old kid buys a book on investing for their mother? That Matthew never stops wowing me. If sports don't work out for our little all-star, I have a feeling he'll be running Wall Street before he's thirty. Heck, maybe before he's twenty.

I'm laughing inside because you just asked me what I'm up to. When I said I was writing a song, you rolled your eyes and flashed me that smile that makes me crazy for you. Well, guess what? I AM writing a song. Maybe I'll send it to your boyfriend, Mr. Presley.

I have a tune in my head, but I don't know notes at all, so you'll have to trust me about how pretty it is. It's a ballad. I think.

<u>Ask of the Lord</u>
Jack Cooper
1961

Sometimes my best isn't good enough,
sometimes I need a little more,
that's why my Father has sent me here,
to learn to ask of the Lord.

When it rains inside my head,
And the drops wet my eyes,
I think of the love that he shared with me,
On the cross, at Calvary.

CHORUS
I must learn to ask of the Lord,
in all that I do.
Yes, I will learn to ask of the Lord,
And all my dreams will come true.

It's hokey, I know. It needs another verse, and according to Sammie it needs a bridge. Maybe someday. And maybe someday I'll sing it for you. The tune really makes it pop to life! (Don't hold your breath, though. The Cubs have a better chance of winning the World Series before I die.)

The truth is I've actually been writing this song in my head for quite a while. I'll finish it eventually, but I'm finally happy with the first part and I wanted to share. I've been humming it for a week or two.

The idea came to me one night right after you first told me about Malcolm. I was sleeping on a cot in one of the secondary maintenance buildings, the one south of campus. I cried and cried—of course you know that already—and the words started to come to me. Almost like a prayer, I guess. I've been writing and rewriting them in my head ever since. I've considered writing them down in a letter before, but for whatever reason I always got caught up in other things and forgot. But not today.

I think I've gotten much better at learning to ask of the Lord. I learned it from you. Along with 3,572,988 other things.

Love you,
Jack Lennon

CHAPTER 23

When Matthew had read all the letters he'd swiped from the Inn's dining room table, the three finished their ride to the truck stop at Tom's Brook with small talk.

They were in no hurry.

Both Samantha and Matthew could think of little else besides their mother's incredible infidelity. Malcolm could think of nothing besides reading more of Jack's letters and discovering who his real father was.

"What was the name of your first boyfriend, Sam? The really weird and hairy and sorta smelly kid who wanted to write fantasy novels?"

"Robert Smith. He's got a bestseller out now."

"Cool."

"And he *wasn't* hairy."

"When did they raise the speed limit?"

"They didn't. And when did you become such a dweeb?"

"Better roll your windows down."

"Why?"

"Trust me," Malcolm answered.

"Will Dad's guy be at the funeral?" Samantha asked.

"Dad's guy?" Matthew asked.

"The attorney."

"Alex Palmer."

"That's him."

"He'll come to the funeral. We'll sign some papers before or after, not sure."

"What happened to the Chevy dealership that used to be on the corner over there?"

"A fire, about a year ago. They rebuilt up in Strasburg."

"Does that crazy, tall skinny guy still run that c-store and bait-shop joint in New Market?"

"His name was Gordon Craw."

"Thaaat's right; we called him Gordo."

"Gordon died."

"Oh."

"Yeah."

"I really liked that guy."

"We all did."

"I'm sure no one cares, but it feels like we're going, like, a hundred and ten. Maybe it's just because I'm in the backseat."

"Shut it."

"I'm just saying."

"Malcolm?"

"Yeah?"

"Don't press too hard." Samantha put her hand on the back of his neck and gently scratched his hairline.

"Press?"

"For answers." She took her eyes off the road and met his. "Everyone is grieving, not just you."

Malcolm looked out his window.

"Don't press, brother, they'll come."

"Wow, boys." Samantha pointed out Malcolm's window. "I swear to you there was a Chinese place right there just a week ago. All the signs are down. Didn't even last three months. That building is bad luck. It just kills restaurants."

"You're right. And you know there used to be a great Mexican place there, Guadalasomething. Mom and Dad took me there for my birthday one year all by myself, not long after we moved up here. I had gas for a week."

"You've had gas ever since."

"You know, Sis, if you're interested, at this speed I calculate we could make it to D.C. in like twenty minutes. Want to—"

"Wanna walk, Matt?"

"Sammie, you remember homecoming the year you made Rain and me dinner and you dressed up like a fancy hostess? I probably never told you this, but between that salad you made, and the trout, which was surprisingly good, well, that was the first time we kissed."

"You and Sam kissed? Oooooooh."

"You sicko," Malcolm answered. A healthy laugh belied his churning, nervous stomach.

"Mal, you did *not* have your first kiss with Rain at homecoming. It was on that church tubing trip down the Shenandoah River. I saw it myself."

"I think she's right, Mal," Matthew agreed.

"Don't you morons think I'd know where and when I had my first kiss?"

"First kiss with any girl?" Matthew posed. "Or first kiss with Rain?"

"First kiss."

"First kiss, my butt."

"No thanks," Malcolm quipped. "I haven't got that kind of time."

Matthew couldn't help but laugh. He wondered when he'd last been so at ease with his brother.

Malcolm couldn't help but think it was pathetic that he knew who he'd first kissed as a geeky teenager, but now didn't even know the name of his real father.

"Okay now, shut it guys, let me order."

"What'll it be?" the gravelly female voice barked through the drive-thru order-box. Samantha didn't bother asking what her brothers wanted.

"Three large Snickers milkshakes, please." She turned to Malcolm in the passenger's seat. "Tonight we're in this together, every single step."

Malcolm thought that was a bit corny, but the gesture was oddly comforting.

She continued, "Now let's go find some answers."

He tussled her hair. "I love you, kiddo."

"Don't touch my hair."

This time they all laughed.

"Pull over," Malcolm ordered as they neared the turnoff for *Domus Jefferson.*

"Can't you hold it? We're thirty seconds from home."

"Pull over!" he pleaded. Samantha obliged and before the cruiser rolled to a stop Malcolm pushed open his door and vomited on the pavement.

"What's wrong?"

"Milkshake . . ." he stammered before heaving twice more. "Milkshake on an empty stomach . . . Plus nerves . . . Bad mix."

Samantha handed him her napkins.

"Sorry, guys."

"Don't apologize." Samantha knew the feeling. She had been struggling with her own feeling of nerves and grief all night. "Shut the door. Let's go home."

Samantha pulled off Route 11 and drove the last three hundred yards up to the Inn. In the bright beams from the cruiser's headlights they saw a man sitting in dark slacks and a blue V-neck sweater on the top step of the porch.

"He made it," Samantha said.

"Who?" Malcolm's eyes were closed and his head rested against the window.

"Uncle Joe."

CHAPTER 24

Samantha, Matthew, and Malcolm each had their own awkward reunion with their father's twin brother on the Inn's front porch. Though it wasn't spoken, none of the Cooper children remembered the last time they'd seen their Uncle Joe in slacks and a sweater. Samantha thought the sweater was probably a large; Joe was a medium. Matthew stared at a tattoo of a license plate number on the back of Joe's hand. Malcolm admired it.

Though they were identical twins, Joe seemed to have a slighter frame than his brother, Jack. He appeared twenty pounds lighter, maybe more, and Samantha guessed even she had more muscle than her uncle. Matthew would later tell his siblings that Uncle Joe's eyes were so alike in color and shape to Jack's they could have been interchangeable. It gave him shivers. All three noticed that Joe's hair wasn't nearly as gray as Jack's had been, though Joe had decidedly less of it. His face was equally weathered, but Joe's sickness was more dangerous than cancer. The bottle had taken a toll.

Joe explained in his quirky, awkward cadence and nervous tone that he'd heard the news about Laurel and Jack on three answering machine messages from his parole officer. Joe had been out all day helping an "old friend" set up a small apartment after an extended stay at the Missouri State Penitentiary and two weeks at a transitional halfway house on the edge of St. Louis.

"I'm sorry you didn't hear it from one of us," Matthew said more sincerely than he meant.

"Do not be. I have not been a part of the family for some time."

"You're a Cooper," said Samantha, opening the front door and ushering the three men into the foyer.

"Thank you very much," Joe said, looking at his feet as he stepped past her.

"Uncle Joe," she pulled at his hand, "Coopers are always Coopers. Doesn't matter how long you've been away. You know that."

"Thank you, Samantha." He paused and stared into her eyes as if there was somehow more to say. "Thank you."

"Have you eaten?"

Joe shook his head.

"Well, come on in. There is enough funeral food here to feed the entire Valley."

"Thank you." Joe followed Samantha into the kitchen where he insisted on preparing his own plate.

Samantha joined Matthew at the dining room table. "Where's Mal?" she asked.

"Changing his shirt." Matthew looked toward the kitchen. "I can't believe he came," he said in a whisper.

"Me either," Samantha answered, "but he's here." She stood and poked her head in the kitchen.

Joe stood at the counter picking at a plate of slices of cold turkey.

"You don't have to eat in there alone," Samantha said.

"It's all right, thank you, your table is being used. I am all right in here."

"Well, come join us when you're done." She turned back to her chair and smiled at Matthew.

He rolled his eyes.

Upstairs Malcolm brushed his teeth and changed into a bright yellow Brazilian soccer jersey. As he descended the stairs he looked carefully at the family photos lining the wall to his right: family reunions; the faces of dozens of guests of the Inn; Jack and Laurel on a pier at what looked like Virginia Beach. His grandfather—Jack's dad—posed with a football and knelt on one knee on a well-worn football field. He wore a leather helmet. Another photo featured Jack and Joe mugging for the camera and sitting on a pickup's rusty tailgate.

"Nice shirt, Pele," Samantha said as Malcolm appeared in the doorway.

"You know who Pele is?"

"I read."

"You read what?"

"Books."

"Books about soccer?"

"Maybe."

"What's the last book you read?" Malcolm took his seat at the table.

"*Tommyknockers.*"

"*Tommyknockers?*"

"I like Stephen King. Angela got me reading him."

"What? You let Angela read horror books? What in the world?"

"She's reading. That's good enough for me—"

"But—"

"—And she likes Clancy, too. She's always been reading well above other kids. Why don't you finish your own book then and give her something better to read?"

"Ah, hello?" Matthew said in a loud whisper; he hoped it wouldn't reach the kitchen. "Can we postpone this little book club for now? What are we going to do about Joe?"

"What do you mean, what are we going to do about him?" Samantha mocked Matthew's dramatic whisper.

"Is he staying here?"

"Of course he is, there's room."

"Do we know where he's been?" Matthew craned his neck toward the doorway and then looked back at Samantha. "Do we even know how he got here?"

"Probably on a spaceship, Matt. Or maybe a prison bus. Relax. He's not a criminal. What's your problem?"

Malcolm, meanwhile, heard nothing. He was already skimming through the letters.

"Don't you think he's trying too hard? He's acting strangely, don't you think?"

"When did you become a judge, Matt? He's obviously upset, probably even in shock. He lost his brother."

"I know that, Sammie, but something's off. Different. I don't know."

"Maybe it's called sobriety."

"Kid all you like, I'm—"

"Hey, Uncle Joe?" she called out, tilting her head toward the kitchen. "Matt wants to know how long you've been sober and how you got to the Inn. He didn't see a car in the driveway."

Matthew dropped his head to the table and banged it firmly three times.

Joe appeared in the doorway wiping his mouth with a paper towel and holding a tall glass of water. "I've been sober since January fifth, three years ago. And I took the Greyhound bus from

Washington National Airport to the terminal in Harrisonburg. Then I took a cab to the Inn."

"Three years? Congratulations, Joe."

"Thank you. I feel good. I feel healthy. I am adjusting."

"Adjusting?" Matthew asked.

"I am adjusting to life outside of jail. I am adjusting to life outside the bottle."

"We think you look great, Uncle Joe. We're proud of you, we really are." She smiled playfully. "But a cab from Harrisonburg? You should have called. We would have picked you up."

"I thought it would be best. With the funeral and everything else you must be doing."

"So when did you get in?"

"I arrived an hour ago, maybe an hour and a half."

"You just missed the viewing, then. The funeral is tomorrow, but we'll make sure you get a moment by yourself if you'd like, before it starts. They both looked so good, so peaceful."

"I would appreciate that. There are things I would like to say."

"Of course. And we'd love for you to come with us, to sit with us at the funeral." She kicked Matthew's shin under the table.

"Yes!" Matthew squeaked. "We'd like for you to come with us."

"We'll ride in the Guthries' limo," Samantha added. "Remember them?"

"Oh yes, I remember the Guthries." He took the last sip from his glass. "Excuse me, please." He disappeared back into the kitchen.

"Let's try harder, please, Matt?" She looked at Malcolm. "You might say something, too, you know."

Malcolm continued reading.

"I think he's got more pressing issues than Joe," said Matthew.

Malcolm read on.

Samantha and Matthew began shuffling through their own stacks, reminding themselves where they'd left off in their earlier efforts to organize them into chronological order.

"I see you found your father's letters," Joe said, reentering the room a few minutes later. "How much have you read?"

"You knew about these?" Matthew asked.

Malcolm raised his eyes.

"Oh, yes," Joe said, pulling out a chair at the head of the table and sitting. "I knew."

CHAPTER 25

For an hour Joe told stories and with each one became more comfortable. More than once he took time to gather his emotions, but before Samantha and Matthew could plunge back into the letters, Joe was launching into a new story about his brother and their adventures together.

Malcolm tuned in and out, continuing to push through dozens of letters, looking for details on his mother's affair and the circumstances that led to his father's forgiveness. After the initial revelation and Jack's sudden trip to Chicago, Malcolm believed that Jack began intentionally writing more vague and coded correspondence. He didn't agree, and he was certain he couldn't have done the same, but he assumed that Jack wanted to protect his mother's honor. He wondered, perhaps hoped, that Jack might have been protecting his own honor as well.

The letters in the months following Laurel's revelation became less emotional and more fact-filled. Some letters contained as little as Jack's diet for the week. He wrote out of obligation, Malcolm reasoned, because he'd made a promise.

"Jack kept his promises," he murmured aloud after reading a particularly uninteresting note written on an index card folded in half and tucked inside a tiny envelope bank tellers used to put cash in for patrons.

Malcolm found no hint of a name of someone who could have been his real father in any of the letters he read.

"I think I best get some sleep," Joe finally said after telling his third baseball-related story. "Is there a place for me here?"

"No question, yes," Samantha offered. "There's plenty of room. One of the upstairs rooms is empty. Top of the stairs on the right, past Mom and Dad's suite. I'd put you there but Allyson has it already. That okay?"

"Allyson is here?"

"Not now, but she'll be here soon, I'm sure. She must have gotten visiting with A&P. Maybe they stopped by her place. You know those two. Mom did a good thing inviting them to become pen pals."

Joe nodded. "Well then, perhaps I'll see her in the morning. Until then."

"You'll find towels in the hallway closet, top shelf. Need anything else?"

"No, but thank you." Joe nodded to each one and then walked

back toward the front of the house to retrieve his bag from the front porch.

"Let me help you." Matthew followed him and kept the door from shutting while Joe bent over and lifted his heavy suitcase. "Listen, Joe, I'm sorry if I've not been very hospitable."

"Do not apologize, young man. I have not deserved any better than I have gotten."

"You're wrong about that. You've obviously changed. I guess I'm surprised, that's all."

Joe smiled. "No more surprised than I am, Matthew. By all rights I should be gone, not your father."

Matthew stepped out onto the porch, pulling the door shut and let the screen door follow. "How so?"

Joe set the suitcase back on the porch and leaned against the front rail to the left of the stairs. Matthew joined him.

"Do you know why I was in prison this last time?"

"DUI?"

"Worse." Joe broke eye contact. "That last drink I had—on January fifth, three years ago—was my last drink because I spent the next two years in prison."

"For a DUI?" Matthew's voice rose.

"More. I hit a little girl that night." He breathed, "I almost killed her."

"But she lived."

"She lived because God saved her."

"That's wonderful then, Joe."

Joe listened as two cars buzzed by on the road at the bottom of the long driveway. "He saved me too. God told that girl to visit me. She came to visit me every month I was in prison. She wrote me letters, too. She wrote me letters almost every week. She even drew me pictures."

"She forgave you."

"She forgave."

"That's amazing, Joe. Really."

"Not amazing. It was a miracle."

Matthew scratched at the head of an exposed nail in the railing. "I wish we'd all known."

"I chose not to tell many people. Your father knew, and your mother, I think, knew, too, but I wanted to leave prison and be tested again before the world waited for me to fail."

"Looks like you passed. You're here." Matthew put one hand on Joe's shoulder.

"I think you are right, Matthew." He looked up. "I did pass. Because that girl forgave."

The two men stood for several minutes more looking out and down the driveway to Route 11.

"Joe?"

"Yes?"

"What do you know about my mother?"

Joe hesitated and looked out into the night.

"I knew your mother well, of course." He hesitated again. "She was wonderful."

Matthew studied Joe's silhouette before finally asking, "Did you know about the affair?"

Before Joe could answer, A&P's Lincoln Town Car roared up the driveway and the men were bathed in the high-beams. Allyson thanked A&P twice for the ride and waved good-bye as the car rolled back down the gravel driveway.

"Is that Joseph Cooper?" Allyson took each porch step slowly.

"The one and only," Matthew answered.

"Hello, Allyson," Joe said.

Before answering, Allyson took the top step and squeezed the thin man in a bear hug. "Your brother was so proud of you."

For the first time all night Joe felt tears drip onto both cheeks.

"Thank you," he whimpered.

"You've come so far."

"Thank you."

"I've missed you."

"You too. I have missed you, too."

She put her mouth next to his right ear. "I'm proud of you, for coming, for everything." She let go and sized up his outfit. "Doesn't he look great, Matthew?"

"He sure does."

"Poor thing." She looked Joe in the eyes. They were wet and

red and tired. "You look exhausted. Let's talk in the morning. You staying here?"

Matthew carried Joe's suitcase upstairs, said good night, and gave his uncle the only hug he recalled giving him as an adult. When he returned downstairs Allyson had joined Samantha and Malcolm around the dining room table.

Samantha turned on their father's record player and spun *Kind of Blue,* her father's favorite Miles Davis album. As the rich final bars of "So What" filled the first floor of *Domus Jefferson,* Allyson handed a letter across the table to Malcolm.

"Read this," she said.

May 29, 1957
Laurel,

I had to go to the train station today to pick up Scott Keebler from Richmond. (He works for the University of Richmond, you met him last year.)

I can't go there without thinking about the day I left for the reunion in Chicago.

I see you on the platform. I see you smiling and waving with Matthew standing by you. He's waving, too. But he's not smiling. I see him looking up at you just as the platform disappears. Of course

I can't hear him, but I think he's asking why I'm leaving without him and when I'll be back.

It was just four days. Why was that so important? Why did I leave you alone? Why did I care so much about men I played a sport with so many years ago when our biggest concern back then was baseball and girls?

WHY DID I LEAVE YOU ALONE?

I only remember one lesson from being a kid in Sunday School. It was about choices. Have I ever told you the train story?

Honestly? I didn't like Sunday School. The chairs were hard and I had a bony derriere. The room was always too hot but we were never allowed to open the windows. They said the Devil could hear us with the windows open. I think there was just too much smog.

So I didn't like the class much. Not then. It was old people telling me things I didn't need to know yet. But one Sunday our teacher, Robert Snow was his name, he was a funny teacher, very smart too, he gave this lesson about choices.

He was the only reason I ever went to Sunday School, now that I think back on it.

He told us about a cross-country westbound train that traveled through Oklahoma City but wasn't switched properly. It was supposed to take its load of something, I forget what, to San Diego. But because of a small piece of track and someone's carelessness, the train ended up in Oregon.

One little choice, Robert Snow said, could take us off on a different direction thousands of miles away from where we wanted to be. I don't know why I remember that story, I just do. Maybe that's not true.

I guess I miss Robert Snow, and maybe Sunday School, too. Just a little.

Today I think about our lives and the day I left you alone. What was so important? I went to Chicago to see a bunch of old classmates and the few ballplayers that didn't come home from the war in boxes. And you stayed with Matthew. You worked. I went to a reunion.

One day. One choice. Something small, but look how it's changed us.

I am so sorry I went. I was selfish. And I am sorry you stayed. I am sorry I wasn't there. I am sorry for all the pain we have all felt.

At least while my choice put us through hell, your choice gave us Malcolm.

I think I'll send someone else next time there's a visitor to pick up at the train station.

I love you, Laurel. I do.

Jack

CHAPTER 26

Malcolm slowly refolded the letter along the existing creases and slid it back into its envelope. He looked across the table at the face of his mother's sister. While Allyson was shorter, rounder, and fairer than her sister Laurel, her eyes, nose, and mouth were strikingly similar. Allyson stood up and circled the table. She tenderly squeezed Samantha's shoulder as she passed her. She stopped at the empty chair at Malcolm's side. She kissed the top of his head and sat down.

"Allyson?" Malcolm said.

Her eyes answered, *Yes, dear?* but her lips said nothing.

Malcolm filled his lungs and exhaled loudly. He slid his chair back from the table. He rubbed his eyes. He crossed his arms and scratched his biceps just inside the sleeves of his jersey.

Allyson asked what everyone wanted to know. "What happened while Jack was in Chicago?"

Samantha nodded. She rose and moved to the open chair

nearest Matthew. The two sat directly across the width of the table from each other. Matthew took both his sister's hands in his own.

Malcolm looked back to Allyson. "Yes."

"This was never the plan, kids." She hesitated. "Maybe there was no plan. I assumed your folks would tell you someday in their twilight years. I know they talked a lot about it, especially since your dad's been sick. I'll admit, I've wondered about this moment. I've tried to picture what it would be like. But in my mind I've never seen myself in that picture. It was always my sister and your dad sitting here." She fidgeted with a small pile of letters. "It's harder than I thought." She tapped the corners of the envelopes, slid them around in a circle, and then straightened them again like playing cards. "This was never the plan. I guess life doesn't always follow a plan, does it? Your mom and dad weren't trying to get pregnant when you came around, Malcolm. They'd been pretty careful, in fact. They wanted to wait another year. Your dad was surprised, but *pleasantly* surprised, of course, when Laurel broke the news you were on the way."

The corners of Allyson's mouth rose slightly. "Jack thought you were an *oops* baby." She looked at Samantha. "Your mother loved you, Sammie, and you, too, Matt." Allyson looked back toward Malcolm. "You all were so loved, so very loved. Your father wanted all of you to succeed more than anything. He was so proud of all of you. . . .

"There is a reason you've all lived your lives so far away from this moment. You must know that. Especially you, Malcolm. You must know that none of this was important because your parents loved and accepted you in the exact same way they did Matt and Sammie. There's no different kind of love, there's no—"

"Ally." Malcolm put his hand on her forearm.

"Your dad didn't have to go to that reunion. He really didn't want to, truth be told, but your mother convinced him he'd regret it if he missed it. That weekend was the first time he'd seen some of those boys since high school. It was the first time he'd learned exactly which ones were still alive. He was heartbroken at how many had died. It only reminded him of what he thought was his greatest failure . . . "

She looked at Matthew. "You went to the babysitter's that night. You remember Mrs. Hatch?"

"I do." He smiled. "Mom talked about her a lot."

"Mrs. Hatch watched you a couple of days a week, I don't remember, maybe three. She lived off Old Lynchburg Road south of town. She watched you while your mother worked at the hospital's pharmacy. Mrs. Hatch had a puny dog, a terrier I think. I forget that dog's name, but she used to yip and yap at everyone like she was keeping the peace. I doubt you'd recall much of that, but Mrs. Hatch was good to your mother. A good friend. She and Laurel kept in touch after Malcolm was born and your mom finally quit working. She was a real good lady.

"That afternoon, the same day the two of you dropped your father off, your mom took you to the Hatches and then went off to work. She had a double shift with only an hour off in between. She worked double shifts a lot because the money was good and your folks were saving everything for this B&B.

"Sometimes your mother stayed at the hospital during that hour off. Sometimes she dashed home to eat and save a dollar. That night she went home for spaghetti. She'd made extra to pack for your dad's lunch and dinner meal on the train. She went inside and ate fast. Your mother couldn't dawdle—she didn't know how, did she?" If it was a question, no one answered.

"When she was done, she lay down on the couch to rest her eyes. It was midnight. She and your dad—and of course you too, Matthew—you all lived so close to the hospital. Four blocks, maybe five. But you also lived around the corner from one of the city's homeless shelters. That made your dad nervous. But Laurel said he was being silly. The men were always so nice on the street and your mother took them extra bread whenever she could. She made such great bread.

"That night your mother fell asleep, bless her heart . . . she fell asleep on the couch in the front room of that tiny apartment.

"Laurel had taken off her coat and pulled it over her. You know your mother wasn't even a pharmacist, right? Of course you knew that. But did you know they made everyone, even the assistants and cashiers, wear those long, white coats? Made everyone look clean. Pure."

Allyson looked at Malcolm and shook her head, her shoulders swaying. "A few minutes after falling asleep," Allyson's breathing and pace quickened. "No one was sure how long it was . . . she woke up with a man on top of her. His eyes were bloodshot and crazy. He pinned her. He ripped her blouse. He touched her." She looked at Samantha, whose mouth was open, her eyes filling with tears. "He forced himself on her," Allyson said quietly.

"No," Malcolm whispered.

"Yes. Your mother was raped."

aped, Malcolm thought. He pictured his mother struggling alone in a dimly lit apartment. A struggle that likely moved to the floor before it ended with the intruder's grisly satisfaction.

Malcolm rushed from the table to the downstairs bathroom and threw up.

Matthew moved to his sister's side of the table and took her in his arms. She sobbed and shook as if she, too, had been victimized. She tried to speak, to ask questions, but the words were choked off by grief and sobs. Samantha had never cried so deeply, with sobs that started in her stomach and made her head throb, not even when she'd learned her parents were dead.

Allyson wept, too, but more softly and for more than just her sister. She wept for Malcolm. Minutes later they heard the toilet flush and then the back door fall shut.

"I'll go," Matthew said.

"No," Allyson stood. "I will." She left the room and found Malcolm swinging in the country-darkness of the backyard.

"I'm stunned," Matthew said to his sister. "I'm . . . stunned. Mom was raped and we never knew. I'm just stunned." He went to the kitchen for a glass of water. When he returned Samantha was poring over letters. "We should wait."

"Wait?"

"For Malcolm. For Allyson."

"Mom was raped. By who? Why? Are we to believe she kept the baby? Are we to believe *Malcolm* is that baby?"

"Let's wait." Matthew returned to the kitchen. This time he filled two smaller cups with milk.

Samantha followed him, watching him from the doorway. "How could you never have known?"

"About Mom?"

"Yes."

"I was a little kid, Sam. I barely remember that house at all. I barely remember the sitter."

"But Mom was raped. *Raped!* There must have been arrests, depositions, a trial. You'd never heard any of it? That seems—"

"Seems *what,* Samantha? You think I knew about this and hid it? Dad didn't know until Malcolm was what—a year old?"

Samantha let herself fall against the doorjamb. "Why wouldn't

Mom tell him? Why would she go through that alone? How do you even hide something like that? How?"

"Dad must've been struggling himself. Mom probably thought she was protecting him."

"So she went through all this alone?"

"She had Allyson, I guess."

"I guess."

Twenty minutes later Malcolm and Allyson reentered through the kitchen door and took their seats at the dining room table. Samantha was on the phone, talking quietly in the kitchen. Matthew was in the upstairs bathroom. Malcolm watched as Allyson rifled through the letters until she found one from March, 1959.

"How did I know where to look?" she asked him. He nodded. "Should we wait for the others?" He nodded again.

When the others had rejoined them at the table, Allyson asked, "May I read?"

Malcolm nodded once more.

March 4, 1959

Dear Laurel,

I don't know how to explain it, really, but I'm sorry I went this afternoon. When will I learn to take your advice?

The hearing room was mostly empty. There were three people from the prison, including Warden Brandenburg, the counselor from the city, and the panel. His court-appointed attorney was there, too. She smiled at me, a half-smile that invited me to come shake her hand if I cared to, but that she didn't require it. I didn't.

They had me speak first, which I opposed, but it didn't matter. I told them word-for-word what I've been telling you for three years. That three years just isn't enough time. There's no way to know if he'll stay away from us, if he'll stay sober, if he'll be any different than the day he went in.

The other witnesses told about his redemption, about how far he'd come, but I don't want to believe any of it. I don't want to forgive. I want him to drink tonight, to make a mistake, to leave the state, to be arrested far away for disorderly conduct. I don't want him to hurt someone else, I just want him to hurt himself.

I want him back in jail for so long that you and I will have left this earth before he sees the other side of the fence.

His attorney said he deserved another chance. She talked about their visits and his journals. He's been memorizing scriptures, and she said he deserves a chance to finish finding God. To help others. To be a man again.

I wish I hadn't spoken first.

I cannot deny to you or God what I saw. He was not a different man, but he is surely changing. When they asked him whether he thought he should be released, he said that he knew he wasn't perfect, he said he'd never be, and that he would make mistakes again. But he said he'd accept their decision and live by it. He cried when he said he was sure that whether in prison or in the world, he would spend every hour of every day of his life paying and repenting for that moment of drunken evil.

Then he said something that surprised me. He said that he'd never again make a mistake that would hurt another. It was compelling. It was, or at least seemed, heartfelt.

Laurel, I want to hate him, for you. That somehow seems natural and right and allowed. I want to see him suffer, balled up on the floor, crying and screaming for rescue. I want no one to rescue him. I want to let him lie there forever.

But at that moment, in that room, all I saw were clean and sober eyes. All I felt as they granted him parole was pity and remorse. He's trying. You're trying. I'm not.

God forgive me.

Jack

I am ashamed, Malcolm. I begged your mother not to have the baby. To have *you.*" Allyson turned her chair toward Malcolm and put her hands on his knees. "I told her it was a mistake to keep the baby and that everyone would understand ending it."

"Ally—"

"No, Sam, he needs this." She looked into Malcolm's tired eyes. "No one, no one anywhere would have judged her for ending that pregnancy. Getting pregnant wasn't her choice and even most pastors would have supported ending it."

"What about Dad?" Matthew asked. "How could she deceive him? Didn't she betray him by not telling him the truth?"

Malcolm studied his brother as he spoke.

"Your mother was afraid. She was afraid telling your dad would fill him with guilt and anger he'd never let go," Allyson said.

"He felt that anyway," Matthew said. "Read those letters—he felt heavy, he felt dead."

"No question, love, but your mother was committed to keeping the baby. She never seriously considered the alternative." She turned to Malcolm. "She believed God sent you," Allyson said. "That He sent *you*, Malcolm, to the earth. You were a life. You were a soul. She wasn't going to end that. She wasn't going to have an . . . She just wasn't going to end it. She believed the choice was not hers to make. Once conceived, you were a life. Period."

Across the table, Samantha lost herself in her reflection in the glass china cabinet across the room. She saw her father berating her former husband, Will, in the living room of their old apartment. She could hear her father chastising him at full volume over the first of Will's two affairs. The second ended the marriage.

Samantha stood. "You know what? If he had known, Dad would have killed that man." She walked around and stood behind Malcolm. She rested her hands on his shoulder and gently rubbed his neck. "Dad would've killed the man. And then he would've gone to jail. And Mom . . . Mom could've lost the baby. She could have lost *you*."

"Well said, Sam." Allyson looked at Malcolm. "And she's right. Laurel knew your father. You all did. He was protective of his family, even of me. If Laurel was going to keep the baby, she was going to forgive the man that took her dignity. And if *she* could, your *dad* could. By the time she told Jack the truth, Malcolm was a Cooper. And trust me, kids—trust me, *Malcolm*—she tried to tell Jack sooner. She struggled with the secret. She wanted to tell Jack so many times before the night she finally did. She and I talked about it all the time. And it was indeed when you took your first steps, Malcolm, just as your dad wrote. She'd been waiting for some sign, some signal. It was your first tender steps that prompted her to lift the burden from her chest. I guess she stepped into the unknown just as you did." Allyson studied Malcolm's expression. "It was time Jack knew."

"Jack Cooper was your father," Samantha said, wrapping her arms around Malcolm's neck. "Every bit as much as he was mine or Matt's. He worked his life for you; he sacrificed for you. He's in your blood."

"Malcolm?" Allyson reached for his hands. "Are you okay?"

Malcolm hadn't looked away from his brother. His mind reviewed the countless camping and road trips Matthew had taken with Jack, the weekends traveling back to Charlottesville, his brother's prized role as eldest.

"Mal? You okay, brother?"

"You knew."

"About this?" Matthew recoiled in shock.

"About *everything*."

"Malcolm. You're wrong, I had—"

"You knew!" Malcolm rose quickly, knocking his chair over and pushing Samantha and Allyson away. He circled the table toward his brother. "Stand up, you liar!"

"Malcolm, calm down—"

"You *knew* I wasn't the same!" He pulled his brother from his chair by his shirt and shook him back and forth. "You *knew* Mom was raped! You *knew* I was different!"

Allyson and Samantha crossed to Malcolm.

"No, sweetheart," Allyson said. "He didn't. I knew. Your mother knew. The police knew. That's all."

"No!" He shoved his brother harder, letting go of his shirt and sending him tumbling to the floor. "You were the oldest. You were always together, you played all those sports and he took you on all those trips because you knew!"

"I—"

"You kept this from me because it made you special!" Malcolm's screams rang through the house.

"Malcolm—"

Malcolm swept his arm across the table in a wide semi-circle, throwing piles of letters flying into the air and scattering them across the room.

"Please, Malcolm." Matthew stood up and stretched out his arms. "I knew when you knew, you have to believe that."

Malcolm knocked Matthew's arms from the air, banging his brother's wrists with his own fists.

Nearly a minute passed before Malcolm caught his breath and looked hard at his brother's face. "You lied."

"No—"

"You lied to me."

Malcolm turned to leave the room and saw Joe standing in the doorway.

"You *all* lied," he said, pushing past Joe.

Moments later they heard Jack's Chevy pickup roar to life. The tires peeled onto Route 11 and the noise escaped northward into the night.

Samantha and Allyson held one another. Samantha shed tears on her aunt's shoulder.

Joe was silent for a moment and then quietly slid from the room and retired to his room.

Matthew, his hands shaking, knelt and began gathering the open letters and envelopes from underneath the table and chairs.

CHAPTER 29

Malcolm drove. He drove north past Woody's on Main Street. He passed the museum, the movie theater, the banks, Ben Franklin, and each of the other Woodstock staples that had greeted him just a day earlier.

At the last intersection within Woodstock's town limits, he made a U-turn and drove south. He parked on the street in front of Rain's townhouse. The shades were drawn and he pictured her sleeping comfortably, alone, at peace, unafraid, perhaps even on the couch where she often dozed off with a book resting facedown on her chest. He thought of his mother. He considered saying good-bye.

Twenty-five minutes later Malcolm pulled away. He watched her windows in the rearview mirror. They remained dark.

Malcolm stopped at the gas station on the corner of Route 11 and Reservoir Road. He filled the gas tank and drove back through town to the Woodstock Tower. He pulled off the gravel road and retrieved a Maglite from the glove compartment and a wool blanket from a cardboard box that had been jammed behind the passenger's seat.

Malcolm walked the short trail, the only sound coming from his feet against the well-traveled dirt path. He climbed the stairs of the tower and sat in the dark. He picked at the paint on the lowest rail, flicking shards off into the night air and following them with the Maglite as they drifted to the ground like snowflakes. After a while, he lay on his back and looked into the western sky until the stars blended together into one bright light.

Birthdays replayed in his mind, year after year, until all he remembered was eating cake on a plastic, kid-sized picnic table in the backyard while Matthew played tag with the neighborhood kids.

Jack watched from the porch.

His mother danced.

"Malcolm? Wake up, Malcolm."

Somebody was shaking his shoulder.

"Rain?"

"Hey there. Sit up." He did and Rain sat next to him, sliding close until their legs touched. She pulled at the blanket and draped it around their backs, pulling on the edge to cover as much of herself as possible.

"How did you know I was up here?"

"Samantha."

"How did she know?"

"She's your sister."

Malcolm nodded. "She called you?"

"She waited, I guess they all waited, for you to come back. When you didn't, she called me. She thought I might be the only one you'd see."

Malcolm reached for the Maglite and watched more paint chips fall to the ground. "Why are you here?" he finally asked.

"Is that a question?"

Malcolm nodded.

"I came to save you."

"From what?"

"From yourself."

"How so?"

"You're an emotional guy." She nudged him. "I didn't want you doing something crazy."

"Like what? Plunging to my death from an observation tower? I'd be lucky to break a leg from this height."

She smiled. "No, you never struck me as the jumper type. I always pegged you going out some other way." She looked at him pensively and said, "Maybe in a boat fire."

"A boat fire?"

Rain laughed. "It's all I could come up with."

Malcolm's mouth curled slightly. He blew hard on a pile of paint chips in the palm of his hand.

"Your sister says you've got something to tell me."

Malcolm chipped away at the paint and didn't look at her. "She didn't tell you."

"A question?"

"She didn't tell you?"

"No."

Malcolm retold the story in a calm tone that suggested the ending no longer mattered. He repeated Allyson's account almost verbatim, but later, when Rain struggled to recall the moment, she heard only the snippets that hurt.

"I thought she cheated . . . Jack stayed . . . Letters . . . The couch . . . Mother was raped . . . Dad stayed . . . The guilt . . . I don't want to know who . . . I cursed Matthew . . . She was alone . . . She'd been alone with it all that time . . . Dad stayed . . . Forgave . . . Mother was brave . . . Decisions . . . Victims . . ."

Rain held Malcolm. She cried on his chest, leaving tear stains in gray circles on the blanket. "I'm so sorry," she whispered. "I'm so sorry."

Time passed and the sun began rising over the Valley.

"Do you remember Senior Skip Day?" Rain suddenly asked.

"Sure I do—I wasn't supposed to be there."

"I was persuasive."

"Yes. Yes, you were." She smiled.

"How many of us were there? A dozen? We climbed Humpback Rock and watched the sun rise."

"Yeah."

"You carried Marge Graves down the trail with her swollen ankle, remember? You carried her, what, two miles?"

"Not that far."

"*At least* that far."

"Maybe."

"You know what's funny? She told me she thought I hated her for the rest of the year."

"Why?"

"Because you carried her, took care of her."

"That's dumb."

"She was sweet. Smart. I guess I stopped talking to her after that . . ." Rain blew into her hands. She looked at the silhouettes of trees in the endless forest before them. "You need to know," she said quietly. She didn't need to look: Malcolm shook his head. "Yes, you need to know. Maybe the man lives here. Maybe it's someone who knew your mother or your dad."

"Why would he live here? No. He was some drunk, a homeless bum. He's probably dead somewhere by now. One hopes."

Rain rubbed her hands together. "It always gets colder at dawn. Why is that?"

Malcolm didn't answer.

"Maybe Nathan can help, or your sister. Sam could probably

track him down from the police records. Find out what happened to him."

"No."

They sat again in the quiet dawn. The mist in the Valley below them slowly burned away leaving the trees beautifully drenched in morning light.

"You remember our first date?" Rain asked, knowing the answer.

"Of course."

"A movie and a tower picnic. My hero."

Malcolm saw the scene.

"You had a lantern up here, which I thought was dangerous, remember?"

He nodded.

"You also had a blanket."

Malcolm smiled.

"You were good to me."

Malcolm looked into her eyes for the first time all night. He moved his face closer.

Rain quickly dropped the edge of the blanket and stood, stretching her arms into the morning air. She shivered. "We should go." Rain carefully began climbing down the stairs.

Malcolm folded the blanket, put the flashlight in his pocket, and followed her down the tower stairs and along the path toward the trailhead and their parked cars.

"At least think about it," Rain said as she opened the door to her car.

"What?"

"Maybe he's changed, like your dad said." Rain lowered her head slightly. "Men change, Mal."

"Not all of them."

Rain sat in the driver's seat and put the key in the ignition. "Will I see you at the church service this morning?" she asked with a smile.

"I think I'll pass," Malcolm answered, tossing the blanket in the truck bed.

"Understood," she acquiesced. "But you'll be there tonight."

"A question?"

"Not really." She stepped back out of the car to hug him. "You're going to make it, Mal."

He breathed in deeply. "Will I?" Her smell was magic, even after half the night on the tower.

"You will."

"Maybe. But without you it'll be a lot tougher."

"You've *got* me."

"No, *Nathan's* got you."

Rain finally dropped her arms. "I've made promises, Malcolm. Promises to him."

"I know." Malcolm opened the door to the pickup and slid in. "I know."

"But like it or not," Rain winked, "you've still got me in the way you need most."

"I know." Malcolm said as he shut the door. He faked a smile, waved with his right hand, and turned the key. He admired—and resented—her honor.

CHAPTER 30

Sunday Morning

Samantha and Matthew were eating breakfast when Malcolm arrived back at *Domus Jefferson*.

"Welcome back," Samantha said as he walked in.

"Thanks."

"Feeling better?" Matthew asked.

"Slightly."

"Hungry?"

"Famished. I feel like I haven't eaten in days."

"You haven't," his sister said, guiding him into a chair. She put a plate in front of him and filled a glass with orange juice. "You're not coming this morning, I assume."

"No, I'm really—"

"Don't worry. We didn't think you would. We'll tell people you needed the sleep—jet lag or something like that."

"Truth is you *do* need the sleep," Matthew added. "I'm

looking forward to a short nap myself this afternoon before the funeral. Maybe a couple hours."

Samantha put hot scrambled eggs and a piece of Virginia ham on Malcolm's plate.

"Hey, about last night . . . I'm sorry. I don't really know what else to say."

"Sorry is plenty."

Samantha bent over and kissed his cheek. "Don't worry about it. You did what we would have done. What *anyone* would have done."

Malcolm looked hesitantly at his brother across the kitchen table.

Matthew smiled back. "Listen to your sister," he said as he stood and pushed his chair in. "Don't worry."

"I just needed to—"

"You needed to do it, to explode, to lose your mind. We saw it coming, my man, let it go." Matthew pulled his suit jacket from the back of the chair. "I'm going to brush my teeth. Ready in five, Sam?"

"In five." Matthew jogged up the stairs as Samantha took a small pill bottle from the upper shelf of a kitchen cabinet. "Here." She put two white pills next to Malcolm's plate. "Take these when you're done."

"What are they?"

"Sleeping pills."

"Mom's?"

"Dad's. He needed them sometimes. Especially near the end."

"Thanks."

Samantha kissed him again and put the bottle in her purse. "Sleep. Ally's already gone to the church with A&P. Joe called Pastor Braithwaite for a ride to Mt. Jackson as well. The place will be quiet. Sleep as long as you can and we'll talk this afternoon before the funeral."

"Thanks, Sam. I will."

"You promise?"

"I promise."

"And Mal . . . no letters. Sleep."

"Like I have energy for anything else." He gave her a faint, if not exhausted smile and began pouring Tabasco sauce on his eggs.

A few minutes later both Matthew and Samantha yelled goodbye from the front door and drove off for the church service and brunch.

Three minutes later a car pulled into the driveway and Malcolm heard footsteps along the gravel path leading to the side door that opened directly into the roomy kitchen. The heavy feet climbed the four wooden steps to the door.

"Come in," Malcolm called in response to the three staccato knocks. The door slowly opened.

"Hi, Malcolm."

"Nathan."

"You're not at the church," Nathan noted.

"I was thinking the same thing about you," Malcolm said.

Nathan ignored him and dropped a small bag on the table near Malcolm's plate before sitting down. "You'll rot your stomach with this stuff," Nathan jabbed, reading the label on the Tabasco bottle.

"If that's what kills me, I'll be in good shape then." Malcolm took the bottle from him and poured another healthy stream of hot sauce across the last few bites of his eggs.

"I hear you've been seeing the sights, for old times." Nathan poured himself a glass of juice.

"Excuse me?"

"The tower."

Malcolm took a bite of ham.

"That's not exactly what we had in mind when we made the deal to let you run loose while you were in town."

"The tower's four miles away."

"Still, you've not been behaving. The deal was you'd stay near Sam and Matt and keep yourself here at the Inn for everything but what was *absolutely* required."

"And staying away from your girlfriend, you forgot that part."

"Fiancée. And I didn't forget. That was next."

"Fiancée? I heard it was on-again, off-again. And right now it's off again."

"That's not accurate information, Malcolm Cooper—fugitive,

runaway, criminal . . . And, in any case, I don't know that it's any of your business."

"It's my business because you lied to me that night."

"Did I?" Nathan spun the saltshaker.

"You weren't engaged. Rain hadn't said yes to you yet."

Nathan spun the shaker again. "You know I love her."

"It shows." Malcolm rolled his eyes.

"We're not that different, Malcolm, me and you. Both strong men, competitive, good at disappointing our fathers. We have different lives, different plans, but we share the same character, don't we?" He spun the saltshaker harder. "I didn't force you to beat that man bloody or to punch me."

"Twice."

"Right," he drawled. "And I didn't force you to take that plane ticket."

Malcolm doused the remainder of his ham with hot sauce, emptying the bottle and tossing it across the room into the trash can.

"I had no reason to stay."

"True then. Even truer now."

Malcolm took another bite. "Why are you here?"

"To deal."

"Not interested. And aren't we supposed to talk on Monday? I want Matt and Sammie here. *That* was the deal."

"That's sweet of you, thinking of them, but we don't need

them for this." Nathan slid the black nylon bag closer to Malcolm's elbow.

Malcolm eyed it.

"Go ahead. Take a look."

"I can only imagine what's in there."

"I only got two years of peace for that plane ticket."

"Take it up with my parents."

"No, no, I'm not complaining. Believe it or not I liked your parents. Good people." Nathan reached over and unzipped the bag. He dumped thick bundles of $20 bills in a pile on the table. "How long does twenty-five grand buy me?"

"Twenty-five thousand dollars?"

"Twenty-five K."

"You're willing to pay me twenty-five thousand dollars to take off?" Nathan had surprised Malcolm before, but the amount was startling and the moment left him spinning.

Nathan smiled and fanned himself by flipping through a bundle of crisp bills.

"So how does this work exactly? I run back to Brazil, or wherever I want to go, and promise to stay out of your life?"

"I figure five years, minimum. By then Rain and I will have a kid, maybe two, and I'll be in Richmond, maybe state senator by then, certainly a delegate. And then you can do what you want with your life. You'll be a speck of concern for me. Maybe less."

Malcolm saw himself returning to the Amazon, carrying boxes of books for children, medicines, water filters. He saw the cover of his unfinished book.

"So I can keep the money and run off and live without you breathing your smarmy breath down my neck." He cocked his head. "Or I can share our little story of conspiracy and bribery with your boss, my sister, Mom's hairdresser—and we let Rain marry whoever gets out of jail first."

"That won't happen."

"Why's that?"

"Because the last thing you want to do is hurt her."

"I'll think about it," Malcolm said, but knew that Nathan was right.

"Think fast, the funeral is tonight."

"I know when the funeral is."

Nathan began packing the money back into the bag.

"No, leave it."

"Leave it?"

"It might help me decide," Malcolm answered.

"Fair. But if you're not in that rental car bound for the airport the minute the funeral is over, I'll have you thrown in the county jail for a month while we take our time deciding how many charges we can file." Nathan smiled coldly. "Breaking probation. Breaking bail. Outstanding property damage charges. Outstanding assault charges." With each charge, Nathan pushed a bundle of bills toward Malcolm.

"Good-bye, Nathan," Malcolm said, sticking out his hand.

Nathan shook it. "Happy Sabbath."

Malcolm swallowed the sleeping pills and loaded his dishes in the dishwasher. He passed through the dining room and saw the letters once again neatly organized in stacks around the table. Samantha, he assumed based on the handwriting, had put a Post-It note on each stack and labeled it with the year. The project appeared to be about a third complete, maybe more. Loose letters and envelopes still filled boxes and file-folders stacked on the floor against the wall.

Malcolm wondered which letter, if any, held the name of his mother's attacker. Without paying attention to months or years, he grabbed several envelopes and climbed the stairs. He took a long look into his parents' bedroom before walking down the hall and dropping onto his own bed.

He read until the pills said *no more.*

October 21, 1987
Laurel,

 I heard a song on the radio a few days ago that made me think of you. More like it made me think of us, our lives, what they mean.

 I liked it so much I sweet-talked Rain into writing out the lyrics for me. (I promised her an extra day off next month in exchange, by the way.)

It's a little folk and a little country, but it's nice and slow. The singer is a fellow named Jason Steadman. I think he wrote it too.

"Nothing Exciting"
by Jason Steadman

We wrote it down on a paper,
a map to the treasure,
hid it down by the shore.

We crossed our steps as we wandered,
we kicked in the water,
you incited a war.

I wrote your name in the sand,
a crooked-heart-dotted "i."
I wrote my name in your hand while staring up at the sky.

We gathered shells under seaweed 'til quarter past nine.
We built a fire with driftwood,
drank tonics with limes.

Nothing exciting, except that I was with you.

We took a stroll on the boardwalk,
ate raspberry snow cones;
I choked on the ice.

I threw baseballs at milk jugs,
I couldn't quite hit them,
we left with no prize.

Jason F. Wright

I didn't notice that mustard was smeared on my chin.
You tried to swallow your laughter,
couldn't hold it quite in.

You held my arm on the coaster,
wouldn't open your eyes.
We headed home with the top down, clouds rolling by.

Nothing exciting, except that I was with you.

I'd seen Old Yeller before,
but this time cried when he died.
I never took time before,
to watch the clouds in the sky.

I didn't realize that mothers
gave helpful advice.
I hadn't noticed some people
are hurting inside.

My life is turning, my world is changing with you.

We bought a yellow toboggan,
you lost your wool mittens,
I started to curse.

I sang a verse of "White Christmas,"
but forgot the chorus,
you made up some words.

You double-dipped in my chocolate
when I looked away.

You look so cute when you're guilty,
I didn't know what to say.

We nearly froze making angels,
but thawed by the fire.
We went to bed at eight-thirty,
though we weren't that tired.

Nothing exciting, except that I was with you.

I'd seen Old Yeller before,
but this time cried when he died.
I never took time before,
to watch the clouds in the sky.

I didn't realize that mothers
gave helpful advice.
I hadn't noticed that lately,
there are stars in my eyes.

Life is exciting, each moment I spend with you.

July 10, 1968
Laurel,

I'm not even going to try describing how this place looks. You'll
have to admire it with your own eyes. It's heaven.

I am spending the night in one of the guest rooms at the Inn at
the absolute insistence of Mr. and Mrs. Condie. They thought I
should experience the Inn at night. I'm afraid it might have closed

the deal for me. It is so calm here, Laurel, a reverent feeling I don't want to lose. I expect when I open the shade in the morning I'll see fog rising in the field below the house and ghost-soldiers marching silently through it. I feel like I'm sleeping in a history book tonight.

I spent the afternoon and evening downtown at a diner on what I suppose is called Main Street. There is really only one street in the town and it runs through the center of everything. It's also called Route 11 or Old Valley Pike, and it goes for miles and miles north and south connecting a whole string of other small towns to Woodstock. I believe Woodstock is the county seat.

This place has some fascinating history. I learned from a woman at the diner named Tiffanee (sp?) about a man named John Peter Muhlenberg (sp?) but who everyone called "The Fighting Parson." Now that's a nickname.

He came to Woodstock in the late 1700s to be the pastor. In 1776, which is just about my favorite year as you know, he delivered a sermon calling for volunteers to join the militia to the Continental Army. At the end of his sermon, he ripped off his church robe and revealed an officer's uniform underneath. He shouted, "There's a time to pray and a time to fight!" What a man he must have been!

The town hosted generals and soldiers from both sides of the war. And one guess who designed the town's courthouse? Jefferson. It's the most beautiful limestone I've seen.

Hon, this place already feels like home to me. The Inn needs some work in a few spots, but nothing your man cannot do alone or with help from Matthew and Malcolm. I see new art for the walls, some new furniture in the rooms, and new mattresses for the cottage. They look like one too many kids have jumped and peed on them, probably in that order.

And it's silly, I know, but I can't wait for you to see the mailbox. It was the first thing I noticed. It's sort of rusty-red with a white dove carrying an envelope in its mouth. It's the kind of mailbox that knows secrets. It's the kind of mailbox that will hold our Wednesday Letters proudly and then beg you to read them aloud. See? I told you it was silly.

We probably don't need to decide for another week, but we can't wait long. The Condies would like to close the sale and be in Boulder within a month, tops.

I could die in this house. It's got to be close to God.

See you in a few days,
Jack

August 26, 1981
Laurel,

It's 3:00 A.M. on Wednesday. How's this for a strange dream?
We were on vacation—Utah or Idaho or Montana, someplace like that—and we were at this B&B and next door there was a general store, real old fashioned-like. It looked kind of quaint, at least from the outside.

So we went in and the owner looked like the creepiest guy I've ever laid eyes on. Then everything we asked for was either out of stock or bad for us.

You asked for eggs and he made a weird "bleh" sound and pretended to spit. Then you asked for coffee, which you don't even drink, and he said, "That's the devil's drink!"

All we saw in the cooler was milk, like that's the only thing the place sold.

I half expected little trolls to come out from behind the counter and eat us. Creeeeepy.

I guess as far as dreams go it could have been worse, eh?

Jack

Almost 150 people attended the choir tribute and brunch in Mount Jackson. Many of the guests stayed to visit afterwards and it was 2:00 before anyone returned to *Domus Jefferson*.

A&P helped with the cleanup until 3:00 and then returned to her home to walk Castro and put batteries in a hundred Maglites. Rain offered to help and followed her home.

Nathan worked in his office.

Pastor Braithwaite read over his remarks for the funeral another dozen times and practiced them aloud, twice.

Pastor Doug sat in the first pew of the chapel listening, admiring, and praying.

Joe walked around Mount Jackson. He sat in a park. He read the *Washington Post* Sunday edition and checked the job listings.

Samantha checked in on Angela at the Godfreys' and then went home to do laundry and take a quick nap.

The Inn was quiet when Matthew and Allyson walked in the front door. They climbed the stairs and found Malcolm asleep in the center of his bed.

Allyson pulled his door shut. "No need to wake him yet. There's time."

Matthew hugged her, thanked her for coming—again—and went into his room for a much-needed nap.

In the quiet Inn, Allyson read and organized letters until 5:00 P.M. when a knock on the front door shook her concentration from one of the few handwritten letters, this one written while Jack was sitting in Arlington Cemetery.

She held open the screen door. "Monica!"

"Hi, Allyson."

"I didn't think you were coming."

"Neither did I."

"You drove?" Allyson asked.

"It's not that far, six or seven hours is all. I enjoy the time to think."

"Bless your heart. And get your little self inside here." Allyson ushered her inside and then held her tight. "I'm so glad you're here." She pushed Monica away from her but kept her hands on her arms. "You look amazing. Just amazing."

Monica wore expensive jeans, a white turtleneck, and a red sweater. Her hair was a soft blonde and shoulder length; her blue eyes were tired but still had a sparkle to them. She carried a legal-sized envelope under her arm.

"So do you. I haven't seen you in forever, have I?"

"It's been some time, Sweetheart, it sure has."

"Samantha called me last night." Monica looked down at her new navy-blue and white Adidas. "My condolences, Allyson, for your sister and Jack."

"They were your family, too. Whether you saw them very often or not." Allyson took Monica by the hand and walked her another three feet through the foyer to the doorway of the dining room.

Monica scanned the room and the years of Cooper history stacked on the table. "Where's Matt?"

Allyson gestured up the stairs with a quiet nod. Monica climbed the stairs and poked her head in each of the rooms before opening the door to Matthew's room and slipping inside.

Six minutes later Matthew tore open the door. *"I'm going to be a dad!"* He flew down the stairs screaming, "Yeaaaaah!" He slid into the foyer on his black dress socks and had to back up to see Allyson sitting at the dining room table. He held up an 8x10 photograph of a beautiful, bald, bright-eyed African-American baby. "This is my son!"

"Matthew, Matthew!" Allyson stood and took the photo from him. She glanced at it again and put one arm around him. "You're going to be a dad. I knew it would happen."

Monica watched from the top step. "And you'll be a Great Aunt—for the second time."

"What's the deal out there?" Malcolm yelled from his bed.

"Get down here, *Uncle* Malcolm!"

Malcolm walked out of the room, rubbing his eyes and saw Monica. He rubbed his eyes again.

"It's me," she said, smiling.

"You're here."

"Yes, everyone seems to be noticing that."

"Malcolm, look!" Matthew stood in the foyer and held the boy's picture up over his head. "Meet my new son."

"Newark went well, then?" He looked at Monica.

"Yes, *finally*. He's ours. We pick him up in two weeks."

"What's his name?" Malcolm asked.

"Good question." Matthew looked up at his wife. "Mon?"

"I like Jack," she answered with a smile.

"Me too." Matthew stared into the baby's big eyes.

"That's great, really great." Malcolm put his arms around Monica and hugged her for the first time in years.

"Sam told me—" Monica whispered.

Malcolm held up a finger. "Not now. This is your moment. Get downstairs and control your husband."

She did, and Malcolm showered and shaved for the funeral of his mother and Jack Cooper.

CHAPTER 32

Sunday Evening

Matthew and Monica rode in the first car alone. Malcolm and Samantha rode with Allyson, Angela, and Uncle Joe in a second, matching black limousine. The two cars passed Woodstock Gardens, the cemetery where Jack and Laurel would be laid to rest later that evening, and cut a smooth trail along the winding stretch of Route 11 between the Inn and Mount Jackson.

Pastor Braithwaite greeted the family at the front door of the church. Also there to welcome them were the Guthries and two other funeral home employees. "Welcome," each of them said, shaking the family's hands as they entered. "Welcome."

The choir sang "Amazing Grace," Jack's favorite song, and Allyson gave a short invocation. From the pulpit Pastor Braithwaite welcomed the congregation, thanked those who'd traveled long distances to share in the life of the Cooper family, and blessed them for their sacrifice. Behind him the Savior Jesus looked down with His arms widespread in a brilliant stained-glass window.

Flowers and wreaths filled the entire front quarter of the chapel. Jack and Laurel rested in their caskets on either side of the pulpit.

The pastor looked down at the Cooper family, lined up in the first pew, with Rain and Nathan sitting in the pew behind. He looked out into a tapestry of faces, some familiar, but many unknown. He spotted Maria Lewia, the Rovnyak family, and Jack's attorney, Alex Palmer, whom he'd met the night before. With a simple nod Pastor Braithwaite acknowledged each of the mayors from the nearby towns who were sitting together with their spouses a few rows from the front. He gave a half-wave to A&P, seated in her customary spot near the back of the chapel. He spotted several restless children and smiled at their parents as if to say, *It's all right, they're God's children so this is their house too.*

He saw his old friend and pupil, Pastor Doug, sitting in the back corner, clutching his own Bible and listening intently. Finally he winked at his wife and his mother-in-law who were sitting in the front row next to the Cooper family.

The long, thin chapel was full. He began.

"Friends, we come tonight not to mourn, but to rejoice in the lives of these two servants of the Lord."

A single hallelujah came from the back row.

"We do not mourn, we praise. We do not cry, we laugh. We do not judge, we forgive, and we count the days until we see them in the resurrection." He continued by reading several verses from the New Testament before introducing Matthew for the eulogy.

"I didn't write anything," Matthew began. "Because I knew I'd struggle to get through it anyway. Words aren't my thing, as some of you know, that's Malcolm's world."

Allyson rubbed the top of Malcolm's hand.

"Now we've learned that was Dad's world as well," Matthew continued.

Matthew looked out at his wife. She dabbed tears and winked with both eyes. "I was seventeen when my family moved to the Valley. Dad wanted me to stay a kid for one more year and attend the twelfth grade and become a Woodstock Falcon. He wanted me to play football one more year." He looked at Jack's casket. "But I wanted to move on, move out. I never worried much about leaving home in Charlottesville because I thought I was already a man by then. I was ready for more. Looking out now, being here this week, meeting so many of you—I know I'll regret not becoming a Falcon for the rest of my life."

"Go Falcons!" someone yelled from the left side of the chapel. Many laughed.

"That's right, young man—Go Falcons." He pulled a hand kerchief from his pocket. "Jack and Laurel Cooper were not perfect people. Dad had a temper, as some of you may have known. And Mother . . . Well, maybe Mother was perfect."

"Amen," another voice said.

Matthew then told several stories, some from the letters they'd pored over for hours. He told of his mother taking Jack's clothes from a swimming hole. The crowd gasped, then laughed. He had the mourners on the edge of their pews as he relayed, with some minor edits for effect, the experience his parents had visiting Graceland while on Laurel's first deathbed.

He pulled a letter from his pocket and read part of the song his father had written in 1961. "When it rains inside my head, and the drops wet my eyes, I think of the love that He shared with me, on the cross at Calvary." Matthew hadn't planned to do it, but he now found himself making up a simple tune and singing the chorus: "I must learn to ask of the Lord, in all that I do. Yes, I will learn to ask of the Lord, and all my dreams will come true." A smattering of applause met his final note.

"Mom and Dad learned to ask of Him. They asked often which course in life was correct. Sometimes those prayers were met with silence. At those times it was because they already knew which path was right for them at that time and place. Other times they were guided to decisions unimaginable beforehand. Those are the ones they've been blessed for. The easy decisions bring short-term relief and satisfaction, don't they?" He looked at Malcolm. "The tough decisions bring everlasting joy. They bring forgiveness. His, yours, mine. The tough decisions bring life." Matthew and his brother simultaneously blew their noses.

"I don't have to wonder ever again whether Dad's headaches are keeping him from sleeping. Or whether Mom is getting enough sleep of her own. I don't have to wonder where my parents are today; they are at His side." He pointed over his shoulder. "I've never been more sure of anything." He looked at his wife. "Thank you. Thank you for coming . . . Amen."

"Amen."

Pastor Braithwaite stepped back to the podium. "At the family's request, we would like to open the floor to any of you who would like to say a brief word. We welcome you to come forward."

Several people did, including a salesman from Philadelphia who had sold the Coopers advertising in a newsletter. "I'd never met them face-to-face," he admitted. "But here I am."

Laurel's hairdresser, Nancy Nightbell, spoke. So did Angela and A&P. The latter wept openly, shaking and struggling for breath as she recalled the Coopers' kindness over the years. "I would not be alive today without them." No one doubted her.

Samantha spoke briefly, thanking everyone for their help during the recent months of Jack's sickness. She thanked Chief Romenesko, standing stiffly against the back wall. She looked at Nathan. "And thank you, Nathan Crescimanno, for your support this week."

Malcolm shifted in his seat, knowing exactly what she meant.

Pastor Doug also spoke. He introduced himself and praised the lives of both Jack and Laurel. He struggled for composure as he thanked Jack for the letters and phone calls on his behalf when Doug was entering the ministry. He marveled at the Coopers' unusually strong marriage and iron love. Lastly he looked to Pastor

Braithwaite, called him "brother," and thanked him for taking him under his wing those many years ago.

After he concluded several quiet moments passed and no one moved toward the pulpit. Finally Pastor Braithwaite stood. "We've been blessed this night, my friends. Unless there is anyone else, I'd like—"

"Pastor?" Joe rose. "May I?"

Joe took his turn at the pulpit and faced the congregation.

"My name is Joe Cooper. I'm Jack's twin brother." There were sighs of recognition throughout the chapel. "I've been in and out of town through the years. Some of you know me. Some of you don't. You that don't are the lucky ones." He gripped the sides of the pulpit until his knuckles were white.

"I've made mistakes," he continued. "I've not been as good as Jack or as good as his boys. I've sure not been as good as dear Laurel or Samantha or any of you." Tears began to gather in the corners of his eyes and run down his cheeks.

"I'm sorry . . . I'm sorry for everything . . . For not being a part of your life. I'm sorry for the mistakes I've made." He began to sob. "I'm sorry for the embarrassment, for the pain I've caused our family. I've wasted so much . . . so much time." He fell to his knees and buried his face in his hands.

Pastor Braithwaite approached and knelt at his side. He wrapped his arms around Joe. "God loves you, Joe, He does. He loves you. He forgives you."

Malcolm's stomach churned and once again he felt the familiar lump in his chest move up into his throat.

Joe returned to his seat and Angela put her arm around him.

"That is the spirit of the Coopers," Pastor Braithwaite offered. "It is unconditional love. I have felt it myself. I have also felt the redemption." He walked over to the organist and whispered something in her ear. She nodded back.

"I think it would be appropriate if we concluded this service tonight by singing, once again, 'Amazing Grace.'"

CHAPTER 33

A fter the benediction, offered with grace and surprising spirit by Matthew's wife, Monica, the crowd filtered into the dark parking lot and began the drive to Woodstock Gardens. As the mourners approached the graveside, members of the choir handed out more than a hundred Maglites. Each person focused the light on the caskets as they were carried from the hearse up a small hill and suspended next to each other on the dark green pulleys above six-foot holes. The combined light created a glow no one had ever seen before.

Pastor Doug said a final prayer and then asked the guests to lift their lights into the sky, each individual beam meeting and combining with the others as the white light reached heavenward.

Members of the family then placed single white roses on Laurel's casket. Matthew put a Ronald Reagan '84 button on Jack's.

People hugged, kissed one another, promised to call, and then the guests left as quickly as they'd arrived, exhausted from a long weekend of grieving.

And suddenly it was true. Jack and Laurel were gone.

The family and a few close guests stood at the side-by-side graves whispering as a single shadow wove through the tombstones and approached.

The figure stopped at the neighboring gravesite. "Excuse me," the man said. His hands were plunged deep in the front pockets of his dark slacks. He wore a tweed sport jacket.

It took Nathan a moment to recognize him in the dark but Rain knew him immediately.

The man approached Pastor Braithwaite and extended his hand. "Beautiful service, Pastor. Well done."

"Sir," Nathan interrupted. "I don't think it's appropriate that you—"

The man turned his attention to Malcolm, his lips twitching in a small smile. "Hi, Malcolm."

"*Tweed,*" Malcolm mumbled to himself, finally recognizing the man.

"Sir, this is not—" Nathan tried again.

"*Sir?* 'Sir' is a little formal for friends, don't you think?" the man said.

"What is he doing here?" Rain asked Nathan.

"I went to law school with Mr. Nathan Crescimanno." Tweed

looked at Rain. "I'm from Winchester. I practice law up in Lees-burg."

"Nathan?" Rain tugged on his hand. "You *know* him?"

Nathan forced a smile and whispered weakly, "I think he's drunk."

Tweed spoke as he walked toward Jack's casket, "I didn't know the Coopers very well. Mostly by reputation. But I heard Jack had been sick." He rubbed his hand along the smooth wood. "Word travels in the Valley." He turned from Jack's casket to Laurel's. "If they were half as good as you people say they were, then they were all right with me."

Nathan stepped away from Rain. "This is not the time, Mull. This is not the venue—"

"Back off, Nathan," Malcolm spoke. "Let the man speak. Or leave."

"Oh now, don't do this, Nathan, don't go all Mr. Common-wealth's Attorney on me. I waited through the whole service for you to stand up and take your turn. I've been waiting for you to feel what I've felt for two years." He looked at Rain. "I've gotten to know shame and regret like I never imagined. I considered com-ing back here a dozen times but never found the courage."

"This is ridiculous," Nathan said. "This man—"

"This man *what?*" Mull interrupted. "This man has a story to tell? You're right." He leaned over and whispered in Nathan's ear.

"This is happening right now. We'll both be free of this tonight. So, you or me? Who will it be?"

Mull recognized the fear and desperation in Nathan's eyes. *"You or me?"* he repeated.

"Malcolm, Matthew, all of you, this man is obviously drunk. He doesn't know what he's talking about—"

"No," Mull looked at Rain and his voice softened. "I do." Weeks and months of guilt lifted enough for the words to take shape. "I attacked this woman two years ago."

Mull took a step toward Rain. She backed away. "It was all supposed to be a game. An innocent game. Nathan asked me to flirt with you, to be a cad."

Nathan fell into one of the folding chairs.

"I watched you in the bar that night and I came onto you. It was just supposed to be a dumb bet between fools, between two stupid, insecure boys." His voice broke. He took a deep breath and looked at Malcolm. "Then I waited for you. I waited for you to show up that night. It was a Friday. It was football night. And you were exactly on time. We knew you'd follow Rain outside, but we didn't know just how crazy you'd react." His eyes apologized. "We baited you."

Malcolm's legs tensed.

"And you bit."

"What's he saying, Nathan?" Rain begged. *"Nathan?"*

"Nathan asked me to have a little fun—but I went too far.

Obvious enough, huh?" Mull walked back to the caskets. "I only meant to have some fun, to get into it, and I made it look like I'd go all the whole way." His voice cracked again. "I never would have, for what it's worth . . ."

"Nathan?" Rain said quietly. "Is this true? *Is this true?*"

No one but his own brother had ever seen Nathan cry. Now he rested his face in his hands and wept uncontrollably.

"Nathan? Did you pay him to do this? Did you set us up? Did you do this to me? *To Malcolm?*" With each question Rain's voice rose and sharpened.

Still sitting, Nathan looked at the ground and wiped his nose on his handkerchief. "I wanted to know," he said too quietly for anyone to understand.

"What?"

"I wanted to know. To know what Malcolm would do."

Rain crouched next to him. "Why?" she asked quietly. "Why would that have mattered?"

The family, A&P, and both Pastors Doug and Braithwaite said good-bye to Malcolm and walked back to their cars, curiously looking over their shoulders as they disappeared from view.

Malcolm remained at the side of his mother's casket.

Mull said he was sorry a final time, Rain and Malcolm both nodded, and Mull walked back through the tombstones to his car on the opposite side of the cemetery.

Rain sat beside Nathan. "Why?"

"Because life with him looking over my shoulder wasn't much of a life at all."

"You didn't trust me?"

"You I trust." He finally made eye contact. "I've *always* trusted you."

"So what did you think would happen?"

"I don't know," Nathan answered, head still bowed.

Malcolm moved toward them but Rain waved him off. He stepped back to the graveside.

"Did you hope he'd let that man . . . ? Did you think he'd find it all clever and funny?"

"No."

"Malcolm loves me, of course he does, and he defended me. Any man would."

"I know."

Rain pulled Nathan's chin around and looked into his wet, pathetic eyes. "You chased Malcolm away."

"Yes."

"You lied to me."

Nathan nodded.

"You *lied* to me," Rain said quietly and turned her face away.

Nathan drove home alone.

The limousines returned to the Inn and, at the request of Alex Palmer, who insisted the family needed to meet for a few minutes that night, the Coopers plus a few friends once again gathered in the living room at *Domus Jefferson.*

"I know this has been a difficult week," Mr. Palmer began as the family settled into the couches and chairs. He pulled a chair from the dining room and sat by the doorway.

Malcolm sat on the hearth, watching the scene unfold, but in his mind's eye was the image of his broken Uncle Joe standing before the funeral congregation.

Rain sat beside him, her eyes sore and red. She twisted a handkerchief in her hands.

A&P and Allyson sat on one couch.

Joe sat in a chair next to them.

Pastor Braithwaite stood in the corner, leaning awkwardly against the wall. Pastor Doug stood at his side.

"It's been a difficult weekend," Mr. Palmer started. Heads bobbed up and down. "I am honored to know your family. Your parents were beyond reproach. Jack Cooper was honest and loyal. I admired him very much. And your mother was a unique, stalwart soul. An example to us all. A miraculous woman. You all know that."

He pulled a folder from his briefcase. "I wish we could have done this another time, but it was your father's final request. In fact he mandated it. His reasons are his reasons." Mr. Palmer held up a file folder. "It's all in here."

Rain took a deep breath and interlocked her fingers with Malcolm's.

"By now you know your father was a letter writer and a prolific one at that." Mr. Palmer reached into the file folder and pulled out an envelope. "Jack left instructions that we read this tonight." The envelope was already open. He pulled out several pages of stationery.

Monica moved to the couch where Matthew sat next to Samantha and squeezed in next to him. Angela sat at her mother's feet.

Allyson slid next to A&P and gestured for Joe to join her. He did. She took both his hands in hers.

Pastors Braithwaite and Doug watched reverently.

"Would someone like to read your father's final letter to your mother?"

"Please," Samantha said, holding out her hand. "I will."

Mr. Palmer handed the letter across the room.

April 13, 1988
My Dearest Laurel,

You have always been a woman of surprises. Tonight you leave me in wonder again.

Here I sit alone, though you are still at my side, peacefully at rest on the bed we've shared for almost forty years. I cannot be alone.

You were supposed to write the last letter, weren't you, dear? After I passed in the night, you were to wake and find me, and you would write the final letter and tuck it away until you could no longer stand to be away from me and you joined me in the skies. And now here I sit alone.

Soon our lives will be history for our three children. An open book, quite literally. I have long suspected that Malcolm will most appreciate the letters. He has always been the wordsmith. Matthew will find them mysterious. Samantha will have to be pulled from them by ten men. She might not sleep for weeks. I hope all three of them will learn from them.

Laurel, our marriage has not been perfect. It has been trying. It has tested us more than we could have known on that day we agreed to this journey. But it has been honorable. I have been upheld by you. And you, you have done that and more. You have kept your promises. Thank you for believing in a greater plan before I did.

I have written many letters and words on these Wednesdays. There is still much to say. But I will see you soon enough. It is the children I must wait on.

I am sorry to each of them that I worked more than I had to. I am sorry that I ever read one more newspaper story than I needed to, or slept one minute longer than I needed to on the morning of our fishing trips. I am sorry that they ever heard me raise my voice. I am so ashamed that I ever raised my voice at any of them. At anyone.

I hope they forgive me for not being the father they were promised.

May He forgive me for my weaknesses. May they forgive one another.

May they be a hundred years away from our reunion above.

Jack

Samantha wiped under her eyes with her index fingers. Matthew put an arm around her and whispered something in her ear. Samantha smiled.

"There are three more letters there, one for each child," Mr. Palmer said.

"I don't think I could make it through another one," Samantha said.

Matthew looked at his brother on the hearth.

Malcolm shook his head.

"I guess it's me." Matthew took the letters and began reading.

To Matthew, my oldest,

You were first for a reason, my son. Your mind and your drive are inspirational. Do you know that? Do you know how much I respect you and am awed by your talents? You were the man given the talents who chose to double them. You have made Him proud. You have made me proud. I cannot wait to see you become a father. You will be a wonder.

Matthew, love your wife. Love her like she's the only one you'll ever have. And she will be.

I love you.
Dad

To Samantha, my Broadway star,

On long days, when I tired of the monotony of the University and the men that did not like to work, I thought of you. I drove home those days, wondering what scene you had prepared for me, what part you would have me play. It never mattered, as long as I could be in the same show with you.

Get back on stage. It's time. Find your light.

I have said it in the flesh dozens of times, and now again in death I say it once more: Sammie, let my beautiful granddaughter know her father. He is not a perfect father, but he is her father.

You shine, Sammie. I would share the stage with you any day.

I love you.
Dad

To Malcolm, my writer, my son,

I have always wondered how angry you would be today. I have cried at night and had dreams of you. I have dreamt of your fury. I pray I'm wrong. I'll understand if I'm not.

I tell you, son, that your discovery is not about who you think your father is. That is unchanged. Since the first time I held you on my lap after your mother's revelation—the day I returned from your grandmother's in Chicago—from that day on, from that day forward, I saw my son. I saw a son who belonged to me and was part of me the same way Matthew was. I saw a gift from God bestowed on me. There was no reason for you to ever know of the night your mother's life changed.

What was true yesterday is true today. I am your father. Your mother forgave. I forgave. Your Lord forgave. So must you.

Malcolm, if you haven't already, please finish your book. Please? Then write another and another. Know that I expect to see you again. And your mother and I cannot wait to see your children. We think they'll look like Rain. You read that right, young man, we've always known what you two have not yet seen. You are meant to be one.

> *I love you.*
> *Your Father*

The room fell silent. Malcolm buried his head in his hands and wept. Rain lightly rubbed his back with one hand and wiped her own tears away with the other.

Only Pastor Doug's eyes were dry. "May I say something?" he asked, looking across the room at Mr. Palmer.

"Of course."

"You may know this already, but I wouldn't be here without your parents." His cadence quickened. "Your dad got me my job, along with my brother there." He looked at Pastor Braithwaite. "There was controversy in Winchester when I arrived. There were dissenters, many of them. I'd been in jail, after all, and some wondered how converted I really was."

Pastor Braithwaite put his arm around Doug's shoulder and squeezed him.

"But you knew, didn't you?" Pastor Doug said.

Pastor Braithwaite nodded.

"I met this man, this fine man, in jail. I spent hours with him. He helped me see my Savior when all I saw was despair and filth. This man, my *brother,* led me here." For the first time all weekend Pastor Doug began to cry.

"Years ago I lived in Charlottesville. I worked as a mechanic. But more than work, I spent my time using drugs and drinking. I even tried to sell drugs for a time but wasn't smart enough. Imagine that.

"At one point I was homeless. I lost my basement apartment when I lost my job at the shop. I spent half the day high and the other half on my face on a park bench. I was rarely in my right mind, or any mind at all. Believe it or not, I used to stay near the hospital because I told myself that if I died on the street I didn't want anyone to have to carry me very far."

Malcolm looked up.

Pastor Doug fiddled with his watch and continued.

"One night, I saw this beautiful figure, all dressed in white, walking home. From a distance she looked like an angel.

"I saw her enter her apartment. I stood outside for a bit. I don't remember it well. I was high and out of my mind. I must have jimmied the door open.

"She was asleep on the couch." Pastor Doug shook and a cutting sob escaped his lungs. He took a moment to catch his breath. "I didn't even see a woman. I don't know that I saw anything."

Pastor Braithwaite squeezed him tighter.

"When it was over," he continued, "when the noise ended, she was in a ball on the floor and I was standing at the door looking up at the ceiling."

Pastor Braithwaite steadied him.

"I walked out the door and stumbled down the street to the shelter. That was the last night I spent in the shelter. I was in jail the next morning."

Malcolm stood. "You?"

"Yes."

"You did this?"

"Yes."

"You're my father?" Malcolm's hands tensed and the veins in his neck stretched tight.

"No, Malcolm. *Jack* is your father."

Pastor Doug stood alone as the others, including Pastor Braithwaite, converged and embraced Malcolm in a warm mass of tears.

Malcolm's tears shook his frame.

Uncle Joe held him.

Malcolm whispered, "I'm sorry."

Rain joined the two of them and they stood in the middle of the loving huddle, their arms wrapped tightly around one another's shoulders.

"I am sorry," Pastor Doug said. "Beyond the simple words I am so terribly sorry. Telling you myself, Malcolm, was a stop on my road to heaven that I could not pass by. Without your forgiveness, mine feels incomplete."

They wept.

EPILOGUE

August 24, 2007

Noah's mouth hung halfway open. He looked at his father. Malcolm continued flicking paint chips into the dusky air and tracking them with his Maglite. They sat a few feet apart atop the Woodstock Tower.

"So Grandpa Jack isn't your *real* father? He's not my *real* grandpa?"

"Of course he is."

"And Pastor Doug?"

"He's my *biological* father."

Noah pulled a handful of pretzel sticks from a bag and stuck three in his mouth. "I'm floored."

"We knew you would be."

"Unbelievable!" His loud voice cracked the night air. "And everyone knows? Everyone in the family?"

"Were you listening to the story?" Malcolm chuckled. "Of course everyone knows. Everyone who needed to know, knows."

"I can't believe it. You say it just like it's old news, like you just read it on some web site and you're just passing it along. 'Hey, did you hear? Your real grandpa isn't who you thought, it's really some pastor who . . .' " Noah couldn't complete the sentence.

"I know it's a lot to take in, son, but it's your history. And it was time you knew. Nothing has changed though. The facts are the facts. You're a Cooper through and through."

They sat watching the paint flakes flutter to the ground.

"Why now, Dad? Why tell me now?"

"Because you're a man. You're growing up and moving on. You're a college student."

"Not until Monday."

"Close enough." Malcolm smiled and threw a pretzel at him.

"And you all *forgave* him," Noah turned toward his father, "like nothing ever happened."

"We forgave him, because *God* forgave him. We don't get to choose otherwise."

"Unbelievable."

"Listen, Noah, it's not as if it never happened. We forgive, but forgetting isn't so easy. You know better than anyone your family isn't perfect." Malcolm connected with Noah's eyes. "This wasn't easy, Noah. We all hurt for a long time."

"Everyone seems okay now."

"Time is a powerful cure."

Noah looked at his father and for the first time Malcolm saw the face of a man.

"What about you?" Noah asked.

"Your mother made me go to a therapist friend of hers in Harrisonburg for a while, six months maybe, just to sort it all out."

"It helped?" Noah immediately answered his own question. "I guess so. You're still around."

"Like it or not."

Noah took a drink from a bottle of water.

"Son, this is history. It's our history. Some of it is painful, some of it is beautiful, but it is who we are."

Noah hesitated a beat and asked, "Can I meet him?"

"Not anytime soon. He died four or five years ago."

"Did you ever see him again?"

"Sure. Your mom and I had lunch with him and Pastor Braithwaite once or twice a year for many years. All part of the healing, your mom said."

"Sounds like Mom."

"He lived well."

"Died a preacher?"

"Died a preacher, a man of God."

"Un-be-lieve-able."

Malcolm put his left hand on his son's shoulder. "Doug White brought more people to God than he could have chased away in three lifetimes. His congregation became a sanctuary for those needing one more chance. He followed Pastor Braithwaite's example and ministered at prisons, shelters. Pastor Doug gave the rest of his life to Him."

Noah went back to peeling paint chips off the tower rail. He borrowed his father's light.

"So what about Nathan?" Noah asked, watching two paint chips race to the ground. "What happened to him?"

"He went to jail, but not for long. The court showed some mercy. We all did."

"And where's Nathan now?"

"He went to Richmond, just like he always said he would. But he never ran for any public office. Got clearance to practice law again on the condition he work as a public defender."

"Did he ever get married?"

"Not that I know of."

Noah ate another handful of pretzels.

"And what about you? How'd you stay out of trouble?"

"I didn't. I got community service, a hundred plus hours, three years probation and a fine from the court for skipping bail the first time. Plus, someone had to take over the Inn. The judge understood that." Malcolm popped a pretzel in his mouth. "Small price to pay for defending the woman I loved."

"And the money?" Noah asked. "The twenty-five large?"

"Ah, yes, the money. Mull left the cemetery that night and turned himself in the next morning for his part in the setup and for lying about it for all those years." Malcolm adjusted his glasses. "We used most of it to bail him out of jail that afternoon. Like I said, mercy worked. And when we got the cash back, we just gave it away again."

"To who?"

"To whom."

"Whatever, Dad. Who'd you give the money to?"

"To the Alan & Anna Belle Prestwich Children's Shelter in Washington D.C."

"A&P?"

Malcolm smiled broadly.

"Awesome."

Noah and Malcolm sat. The evening sky darkened and the stars slowly appeared.

"What about the other letter?"

"What other letter?" Malcolm swiveled his head toward Noah.

"The one from Mom. The one she wrote you while you were in Brazil. The one you said you never got."

"Ahhh. Thought I'd slipped that one by you. My son, the genius."

"You lied to her about not getting the letter, didn't you?"

"Maybe."

"So you had it the whole time?"

"Maybe."

"You did!" Noah punched his dad's arm. "Did you read it?"

"Maybe."

"What did it say?"

"Sorry, Genius, you're going to have to ask your mother about that."

Malcolm gingerly transferred a large pile of paint chips to Noah's open palm.

Noah blew hard on them, sending them between two rails of the balcony and into the air.

Malcolm's eyes followed a single white piece as it floated to the ground.

He didn't see it land.